Co-eternals

A STORY OF ENTANGLED CONSCIOUSNESS

SALLY SULFARO

Sequel to

The Antiheroes
Treatise of a Lost Soul

by Abe Sulfaro

United States Copyright Office Registration Number: TXu 2-085-884

First Edition

ISBN-13: 978-1-946274-25-0
eBook - ISBN-13: 978-1-946274-26-7

Cataloging-in-Publication data available from Library of Congress

Published in the United States by Wordeee 2019

Website: www.wordeee.com
Twitter: wordeeeupdates
Facebook: Wordeee
E-Mail: contact@wordeee.com

Cover Design and Layout: Amit Dey
Cover photo is a passageway leading to Piagnaro Castle, Pontremoli, Italy. (Photo: Sally Sulfaro)

Dedication

TO MY HUSBAND MICHAEL with gratitude and love. Your presence is my home.

To our sons, Abe (1970 - 2014), Detroit rock musician, poet, and author of *The Antiheroes: Treatise of a Lost Soul* and *Memoirs de Nocturne: An Anthology* and Josh, guitarist, composer, and wayfarer. You are Moonbeams and Sunlight, miraculous muses, my inspiration and my reason.

To the medieval town of Pontremoli and the village of San Cristoforo in the enchanted region of Lunigiana, Land of the Moon. The hospitality and warmth of your people have touched our family in unforgettable ways.

Acknowledgements

J OSH AND HEATHER SULFARO, in your grief, you were led to Lunigiana and the stone farmhouse, a sanctuary beside the Cappella dei Pellegrini (Chapel of the Pilgrims) on the ancient Via Francigena.

Dr. Paulette Moulton; Lana Hammac; Jennifer Bellestri Rimanelli, Nurse Practitioner; Dr. Vincent Rimanelli; Greg (Spam) McFarland; Marty Fitrzyk; Dayve (Disintegration) Watson; Jess Allera; Beverly Messineo; Carrie Lambert; Jim and Royetta Doe

With us during our darkest hours, you gave Abe loving support and the best care he could have received anywhere. Your kind ways inspire everyone you touch.

Ryan Sulfaro

Once again, your art has enhanced our family's written work. All the artwork in *Co-eternals* was created by Ryan.

Contents

Timelines: Pops, Kings, Archbishops & Novel Characters

*POPES

| John XII 955-964 | Antipope Leo VIII 963-964 | Benedict V 964 [1 month] | John XIII 965-972 | Benedict VI 973-974 | Antipope Boniface VII 974,984-985 | Benedict VII 974-983 | John XIV 983-984 | John XV 985-996 |

*KINGS OF THE ENGLISH

| Edgar the Peaceable 959-975 | Edward the Martyr 975-978 | Æthelred the Unready 978-1016 |

*ARCHBISHOPS OF CANTERBURY

| Dunstan 960-988 | Æthelgar 988-990 | Sigeric 990-994 |

Cynewyn
b. 933, d. 963

Ead
b. 930, d. 990

Bath Abbey

Maffeo (Feo)
b. 963, d. 990
Glastonbury Abbey

Fastrada
b. 965, d. 990
San Cristoforo, Italy

Epifano (Fano), b. 1968
Pontremoli, Italy

Fade (Abe), b. 1970, d. 2008
Detroit, Michigan, USA

Carnival (Niv), b. 1973
Detroit, Michigan,
Pontremoli, Italy

*Historical information on the next 6 pages.

*Historical Information on Popes, Kings of the English, and Archbishops of Canterbury

POPES:

❖ John XII (955 – 964 A.D.)

John served in dual roles as secular prince of Rome and spiritual head of the church with leanings toward the secular. He has been described as a coarse, immoral man. It was during his papacy that the Lateran Palace was spoken of as a brothel and corruption in Rome became a general disgrace. He was assassinated in Rome in 964.

❖ Antipope Leo VIII (963 – 964 A.D.)

Leo opposed John XII and Benedict V. There were at least 37 antipopes between 217 and 1439 A.D. when papal elections were obscured by incomplete and biased records. Some popes were not elected but were aristocrats who purchased the position. Antipopes made significantly accepted claims to be Pope, Bishop of Rome, and leader of the Catholic Church in opposition to the person who was otherwise considered to be legitimately elected.

❖ Pope Benedict V (May 22 – June 23, 964 A.D.)

Benedict V was Pope for a very brief time (one month). He opposed Antipope Leo VIII. His pontificate was at the end of a dark period known as the Saeculum Obscurum, also known as the Pornacracy or the Reign of the Harlots, a sixty-year era during which popes were strongly influenced by the powerful and corrupt Theophylacti family. Benedict was overthrown by Emperor Otto I after a violent struggle between rivaling factions that resulted in famine when land surrounding Rome was ravaged. Benedict was brought before a synod convened by the Antipope Leo VIII, accused of breaking an oath to Emperor Otto I never to elect a pope without consent, and told he would be allowed to live if he would admit his guilt and throw himself at the mercy of Leo. Benedict did so. He was allowed to retain deacon status and was exiled to Hamburg, Germany.

❖ John XIII (965 – 972 A.D.)

John was the son of a bishop and was raised in the Lateran Palace. He was a member of the Schola Cantorum, the trained papal choir specializing in plainchant (monophonic chants consisting of a single melodic line used in liturgies of the Western Church). John was known for his piety and reverence and was schooled in scripture as well as canon law. His nickname was the White Hen because of his light-colored hair. This pontificate was defined by an ongoing conflict between Emperor Otto I and the Roman nobility.

❖ Pope Benedict VI (973 – 974 A.D.)

Benedict VI was imprisoned in Castel Sant' Angelo and put to death by Anitpope Boniface VII (below) during the establishment of the Holy Roman Empire and the transition between German Emperors Otto I and Otto II. Otto

II's distraction with the death of Otto I allowed power struggles between aristocratic Roman families (Crescentii and Tusculani) to crop up. When Otto II sent an emissary to demand Benedict's release from prison, Boniface ordered Benedict's death. Benedict was strangled by a priest named Stephen.

❖ Antipope Boniface VII (974, 984 – 985 A.D.)

A tumult among the populace, possibly over the death of Benedict VI, compelled Boniface (Cardinal-Deacon Franco Ferrucci, preferred candidate of the Crescentii family and the anti-German faction) to flee to Constantinople in 974, carrying away a vast treasure. He returned in 984 and removed John XIV (see below). Little is known of this 11-month papacy, but there is clear history of public disgust. His body was dragged through the streets of Rome, stripped naked, and dumped beneath the statue of Marcus Aurelius in front of the Lateran Palace. It is probable that he committed many atrocities in retaliation for his previous exile. He was called *horrendum monstrum* (horrible monster) and referred to as *Malefatius* (Mal meaning "bad") rather than Bonifatius.

❖ Benedict VII (974 – 983 A.D.)

Benedict faced strong opposition from the followers of Boniface VII even after he fled to Constantinople, forcing Benedict to seek the support of Emperor Otto II. Once firmly established as pope, Benedict worked against the tide of simony (buying and selling of ecclesiastical privileges) and advanced monasticism.

❖ Pope John XIV (983 – 984 A.D.)

John XIV was imprisoned in Castel Sant'Angelo in Rome by Antipope Boniface VII and died there, either by poisoning or starvation.

❖ Pope John XV (985 – 996 A.D.)

John XV was unpopular because of his nepotism and venality. He divided the papal treasury among his relatives. He was the first pope to canonize a saint in 993. Before that time, saint cults were local.

KINGS OF THE ENGLISH:

❖ Edgar the Peaceable (959 – 975 A.D.)

Edgar inherited the throne as a teenager following the death of his elder brother, Eadwig. His reign was noted for stability. His most trusted advisor was Dunstan whom he appointed Archbishop of Canterbury.

❖ King Edward the Martyr (975 – 978 A.D.)

Edward was the eldest son of King Edgar the Peaceable, but he was an unacknowledged heir. He became king at the age of 15 or 16 following the death of his father. He is believed to have been murdered at the request of his stepmother, Queen Dowager Ælfthryth, and replaced by her son and Edward's half-brother, Æthelred, who was 12 years old. Edward's assassination resulted in his veneration, and he was considered a saint shortly after his death.

- ❖ King Æthelred the Unready (978 – 1016 A.D.)

  Youth (crowned at 12 years of age) and poor judgment led to Æthelred being known as Æthelred the Unready, not to mention that general suspicion around the death of his half-brother, King Edward, cast a dark shadow over his reign. England was plagued by conflict with the Danes. Based on advice from Sigeric, Archbishop of Canterbury, Æthelred paid the Danes not to invade English territory. Doing so set a precedent that resulted in further financial burdens on the English people with even Sigeric subsequently having to pay the Danes in order to avert the burning of Canterbury Cathedral.

ARCHBISHOPS OF CANTERBURY:

- ❖ Dunstan (960 – 988 A.D.)

  Dunstan served as minister of state to several English kings and was the most popular saint in England for almost two centuries. As a child, he studied under Irish monks within the ruins of Glastonbury Abbey. He mastered artistic craftsmanship, was tonsured (crown of the head shaven), and served in the ancient church of St. Mary. He was appointed to the court of King Athelstan where he became a favorite. A plot to disgrace him accused him of black magic, and the king ordered him to leave his court. As he exited the palace, he was attacked, beaten, bound, and thrown into a cesspool. He escaped to Winchester where he entered the service of his uncle, the Bishop of Winchester. It was there that Dunstan experienced tumors all over his body, thought by some to be leprosy but more likely caused by an infection after being thrown into the cesspool. He had previously believed he did not have the inclination to lead a celibate life, but the tumors changed his mind. He returned to Glastonbury and lived the life of a hermit monk at the church of St. Mary in a small cell where he studied, worked at handicrafts, and played harp. According to legend, it was here that he was tempted by the devil whom Dunstan held by the face with tongs. He later served as Abbot of Glastonbury Abbey, Bishop of Worcester, Bishop of London, and Archbishop of Canterbury. He is credited with the restoration of monastic life in England and reformation of the English Church. He was canonized as a saint in 1029.

❖ Æthelgar (988 – 990 A.D.)

Æthelgar was a monk at Glastonbury Abbey before becoming Bishop of Winchester, continuing as a monk at Abingdon Abbey and later appointed Abbot of New Minster, a newly reformed monastery. He was then consecrated Bishop of Selsey and finally succeeded Dunstan as Archbishop of Canterbury. His was a fairly uneventful tenure as Archbishop, the most notable events being receipt of requests for support from monasteries in Flanders.

❖ Sigeric or Sigerico (990 – 994 A.D.)

Known as "Sigeric the Serious," he was educated at Glastonbury Abbey and served as Abbot of St. Augustine's Abbey and Bishop of Ramsbury before becoming Archbishop of Canterbury. His pilgrimage to Rome on the Via Romea (Via Francigena) in 990 A.D. was the first to be charted.

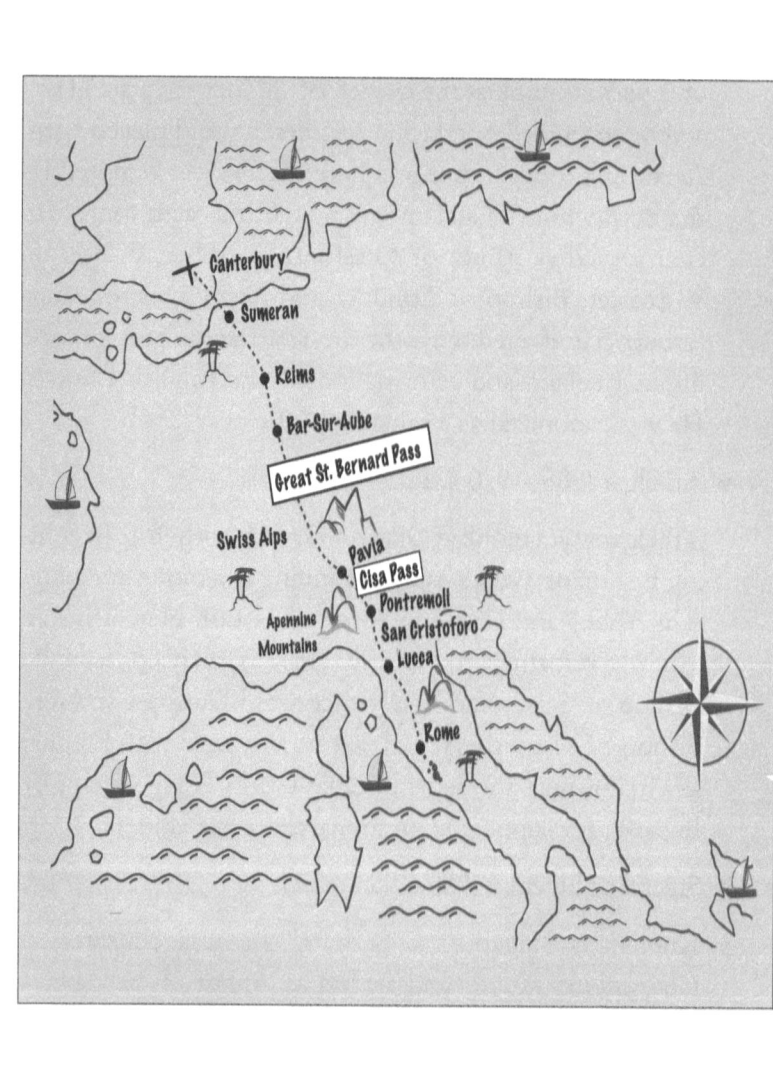

Stages on the Via Romea (Via Francigena)

Roads to Rome from various locations in Europe passed through France, Switzerland, and Italy. A route was not clearly described prior to 990 A.D. and the journey of Sigeric, Archbishop of Canterbury, even though pilgrims had made the trip for several hundred years. There were multiple routes, hence the saying, "All roads lead to Rome." For example, there were three or four possible crossings of the Alps and the Apennines. Sigeric's itinerary described 80 stops or stages between the English Channel and Rome, Italy covering 1,900 kilometers (1,180.6 miles). The stages were originally numbered in reverse order (on the return trip) from Rome. Since then, the stages have been numbered from 1 to 80 in both directions beginning and ending with crossing the English Channel.

Stage	Place Name on Sigeric's Itinerary	Present Place Name
1	Sumeran	Sombre (in Wissant), France
2	Name of stage is missing	
3	Gisne	Guines, France
4	Teranburh	Therouanne, France
5	Bruwaei	Bruay-la-Buissiere, France
6	Atherats	Arras, France
7	Duin	Doingt, France
8	Martinwaeth	Seraucourt-le-Grand, France

Stage	Place Name on Sigeric's Itinerary	Present Place Name
9	Mundlothuin	Laon, France
10	Corbunei	Corbeny, France
11	Rems	Reims, France
12	Chateluns	Chalons-en-Champagne, France
13	Funtaine	Fontaine-sur-Coole, France
14	Domaniant	Donnement, France
15	Breone	Brienne-le-Chateau, France
16	Bar	Bar-sur-Aube, France
17	Blaecuile	Blessonville, France
18	Oisma	Humes-Jorquenay, France
19	Grenant	Grenant, France
20	Sefui	Seveux, France
21	Cuscei	Cussey-sur-l'Ognon, France
22	Bysiceon	Besancon, France
23	Nos	Nods, France
24	Punterlin	Pontarlier, France
25	Antifern	Yverdon-les-Bains, Switzerland
26	Urba	Orbe, Switzerland
27	Losanna	Lausanne, Switzerland
28	Vivaec	Vevey, Switzerland
29	Burbulei	Aigle, Switzerland
30	Sce Maurici	Saint-Maurice, Switzerland

Stage	Place Name on Sigeric's Itinerary	Present Place Name
31	Ursiores	Orsieres, Switzerland
32	Petrecastel	Bourg-Saint-Pierre, Switzerland
33	Sce Remei	Saint-Rhémy-en-Bosses, Italy
34	Agusta	Aosta, Italy
35	Publei	Pont-Saint-Martin, Italy
36	Everi	Ivrea, Italy
37	Sca Agatha	Santhià, Italy
38	Vercel	Vercelli, Italy
39	Tremel	Tromello, Italy
40	Pamphica	Pavia, Italy
41	Sce Cristine	Santa Cristina e Bissone, Italy
42	Sce Andrea	Corte San Andrea, Italy
43	Placentia	Piacenza, Italy
44	Floricum	Fiorenzuola d'Arda, Italy
45	Sce Domnine	Fidenza, Italy
46	Metane	Costamezzana (Medesano), Italy
47	Philemangenur	Fornovo di Taro (Felegara), Italy
48	Sce Moderanne	Borceto, Italy
49	Sce Benedicte	Montelungo, Italy
50	Puntremel	Pontremoli, Italy
51	Aguilla	Aulla, Italy

Stage	Place Name on Sigeric's Itinerary	Present Place Name
52	Sce Stephane	Santo Stefano di Magra, Italy
53	Luna	Luni, Italy
54	Campmaior	Pieve di Camaiore, Italy
55	Luca	Lucca, Italy
56	Forcri	Porcari, Italy
57	Aqua Nigra	Ponte a Cappiano (Fucecchio), Italy
58	Arne Blanca	Fucecchio, Italy
59	Sce Dionisii	San Genesio (San Miniato), Italy
60	Sce Peter Currant	Coiano (Castelfiorentino), Italy
61	Sce Maria Glan	Santa Maria a Chianni near Gambassi Terme, Italy
62	Sce Gemiane	San Gimignano, Italy
63	Sce Martin in Fosse	San Martino Fosci, Italy
64	Aelse	Gracciano, Italy
65	Burgenove	Badia a Isola (Monteriggioni), Italy
66	Seocine	Siena, Italy
67	Arbia	Ponte d'Arbia (Monteroni), Italy
68	Turreiner	Torrenieri (Montalcino), Italy
69	Sce Quiric	San Quirico d'Orcia, Italy
70	Abricula	Briccole di Sotto, Italy

Stage	Place Name on Sigeric's Itinerary	Present Place Name
71	Sce Petir in Pail	San Pietro in Paglia (Voltole), Italy
72	Aquapendente	Aquapendente, Italy
73	Sca Cristina	Bolsena, Italy
74	Sce Flaviane	Montefiascone, Italy
75	Sce Valentine	Viterbo (Bullicame), Italy
76	Furcari	Vetralla (Forcassi), Italy
77	Suteria	Sutri, Italy
78	Bacane	Baccano (Campagnono di Roma), Italy
79	Johannis VIII	San Giovanni in Nono (La Storta), Italy
80	Urbs Roma	Roma, Italy

In Lieu of a Foreword

The long and winding road that leads to your door
Will never disappear, I've seen that road before
It always leads me here, leads me to your door
The wild and windy night that the rain washed away
Has left a pool of tears, crying for the day
Why leave me standing here? Let me know the way

The Long and Winding Road
Paul McCartney

Sometimes I go about pitying myself
and all along my soul is being blown
by great winds across the sky.

Ojibwa Saying

If in the twilight of memory we should meet once more,
we shall speak again together and you shall sing
to me a deeper song.

Kahlil Gibran

Introduction

WE SAW HIM ONE SUMMER MORNING in 2016 as we were sitting in the sun at the Piazza della Repubblica, Pontremoli, Italy. My daughter-in-law, Heather, first noticed him standing near the Comune. His resemblance to Abe, the older of my two sons, Detroit rock musician, author, and poet who died in 2014, was striking. We have seen this man in Pontremoli many times since, and each time I've had to pinch myself. So began this story.

Co-eternals is not a story I intended to write but rather a narrative that was passed by unseen hands to a perpetually grieving mother. Oscar Wilde wrote, "Where there is sorrow, there is holy ground." Only now can I grasp the truth in his words. It's as if an aura surrounds our family since Abe's death, others sensing our deep sorrow and supporting us with exactly what is needed at just the time it is needed. Similarly, the story and underlying concepts in *Co-eternals* surfaced as if channeled from an unknown source. Perhaps these gifts are the result of synchronicity, heightened sensitivity, or just happenstance, but I don't think so.

This story reaches out to a dimension where consciousness travels between one flesh-bound existence and another. Hope for unending consciousness is intensified by the loss of someone so dear that one's total being cries out for any indication of continual existence and an eternal bond, ergo the characters in this story are not souls adrift in a sea of coincidental earthly harbors. They are wayfarers in purposeful search of resolutions to pursuits and yearnings, leaving each lifetime here—sometimes to continue an unfinished cycle of consciousness and other times to transcend—always in pursuit of an ideal state of consciousness and with perpetual dangling entanglements.

Sections and quotes from *The Antiheroes: Treatise of a Lost Soul* and writings from *Memoirs de Nocturne: An Anthology*, both written by Abe and published posthumously, are used in this book to connect characters, places, and concepts. In many ways, Abe's life and writings were the catalysts for this tale that bridges centuries and continents trailing entangled souls. Dr. Paulette Moulton was the other provocative influence. As I struggled with the loss of my son, sorrowfully contemplating where he is, she gently counseled, "Pay attention." So, Paulette, dear friend and sister, I continue to pay attention.

I hope readers will find comfort and relevance, or at least cause to ponder, within these pages.

Sally Sulfaro

Pre-Sequel Background

A T THE END OF *THE ANTIHEROES*, the main character Fade and his girlfriend, Niv, have been brutally assaulted by Niv's ex-husband and his corrupt cop comrades, left for dead in the loft of the abandoned building where Fade lives. After waking up in a pool of blood from a gunshot wound to the head that turns out to be a deeply grazed scalp, Fade finds Niv badly beaten and unresponsive, appearing dead. His dog, Vader, has been shot and killed. Fade summons his small group of friends, [1]Goth rogues whose home base is Detroit's infamous City Club in the Leland Hotel, and persuades them to accompany him on a mission of revenge at the Lincoln Bar, a known hangout for crooked Detroit cops. The Lincoln is full of them when Fade, Spam, Keith, and John arrive and open fire. There are no survivors, Fade alone making it back to the loft to release his death muse, the Black Rabbit, and lie down to die beside Niv. As he dies, Fade hears echoes of a distant past, the chanting of monks, and has a premonition that his most treasured possessions, his journal and prose, will find their way into the hands of a contemporary, an unknown kindred soul...all the while hearing his given name, Abe, emanating from an unknown source—the Black Rabbit?

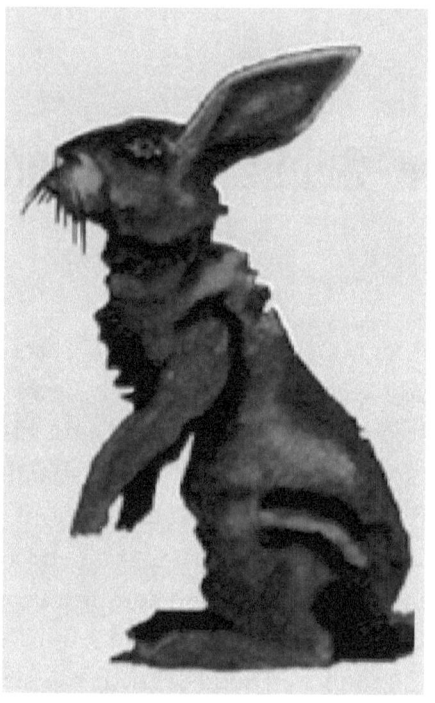

Italics are used in this novel to indicate a character's thoughts.

This work of fiction contains references to real places and historical events.

Superscript [1,2,3] numbers correspond with annotations at the end of the book.

The annotations contain historical facts and information that may be interesting or helpful to the reader, particularly in regard to towns and villages along the Via Romea, also known as the Via Francigena, popes, kings, and the relationship between church and state during the tenth century.

ONE

18 July 2010,
¹Pontremoli, Italy

Fade Away

NIV GASPS, HER HEART RACING AS she catches a glimpse of him standing in front of the *Comune in the Piazza della Repubblica* on a sunny mid-July morning. She closes her eyes and reopens them, certain the apparition will have vanished. No. He's there, black shoulder-length hair, sunglasses pushed up above his forehead, wearing loose-fitting white cotton trousers and a stylish white thigh-length tunic. The resemblance is uncanny and yet he's different. Fade died in Detroit two years ago. Besides, Fade was Goth to the core and would never wear any color except black, and he definitely wouldn't be out in the sunshine, or out *anywhere* for that matter, this early in the day.

Get a freakin' grip, Niv. You're in Italy and Fade is dead. Too much vino last night? Or perhaps it's the lingering effects of brain trauma?

A woman approaches him and they begin to talk. Of course. Women were always drawn to Fade's exotic good looks, men to his alpha male charisma. This beautiful man's aura is unmistakable. Niv finds herself thinking it just might be possible…

entangled consciousness. She should have died with Fade in Detroit but somehow survived the ruthless assault by her ex-husband and his lawless band of cops. As she's struggling internally about whether to approach the man in the piazza, he walks away toward Via Garibaldi in the direction of the streets leading uphill to Pontremoli's historic fortress, [2]*Castello del Piagnaro.*

No, I will not chase after him only to discover that he's not Fade, embarrassing myself and causing him to think I'm a wing-nut stalker. After all, I'm here to try to move forward with my life, to put the past in perspective and piece together a make-due existence after losing the one great love of my life. Any interaction with someone who merely resembles Fade cannot help me toward that end.

In this reality-check moment, Niv recalls Fade's words about the sought after and revered human state known as love, a state he acknowledged but would never commit to. "Mortality by its very nature renders all love tragic." His insights always transcended current circumstances, as if he had amassed experience and wisdom across multiple lifetimes. There were times when he seemed ready and even eager to move on to his next incarnation or, as he preferred to describe it, the next cycle of consciousness. He had an expectation, actually a certainty, of his early demise, symbolized by his death muse, the [3]Black Rabbit. Without a doubt he had a death wish on that last night in Detroit, diving headlong with his tight-knit squad of [4]Goths into a bar packed with murderous rogue cops who believed they had killed Fade, his dog Vader...and me.

TWO

2008 Detroit, Michigan

The Black Rabbit's Call

FADE SCANS THE HUGE DANCE floor at [1]City Club, Goth home territory, looking for Niv. She's sure to be here tonight. He has become increasingly concerned because she's been asking a lot of questions about his past as well as his present life. Sharing the details of his family and upbringing with another human being is almost impossible for him. It would be an intrusion into guarded quarters...an intimacy he can't afford psychologically or emotionally. An even more threatening thought is that allowing Niv to look into his past would make her want to comfort and heal his scarred spirit. Worse yet, it would cause him to feel a deep connection with this wonderful person Niv, an anchor he can't abide.

It's probably a mistake to think I can hide anything from her. She seems to know things about me without ever being told. She must be a witch...a good witch, I hope.

Fade pauses in this conversation with himself to deal with opposing internal forces.

Nope. Can't afford to make myself vulnerable, not even with her. Never have and never will. I often wonder what it is, even aside from Niv… this eerie sense of a distant past and a personal history that has caused my disdain for religion and rejection of social norms. It was especially keen when I was a kid, unfortunately born into an environment that could only feed a pre-existing revulsion, almost as if there is a past beyond this life's past. Now that I've met Niv, the shadowy recall of a distant past returns more frequently in brief flashes. It feels like she was there with me then and is now a channel, a connection to a time I can't actually recall although I'm certain of it.

Retreating to the dark platform at the back of the dance floor, Fade hopes to shake off unwanted memories of his childhood. It seems appropriate that they're playing the song "This Wreckage" by Gary Numan. A sickening feeling washes over him as he recalls his given name, Abe, and his upbringing by a stern, misguided mother and a father who was mostly absent, a coping strategy that might have been in his own best interest but amounted to abandonment of his only child. He worked at Ford Motor Company, an hourly production-line job, seven days a week and spent most evenings in bars with his buddies to avoid the joyless, tense environment at home, leaving the raising of his son to a pathologically Baptist wife whose grandparents had migrated north in the 1930s in search of work, leaving the area around the Powell River in eastern Tennessee. Detroit's factories and steel mills provided an economic setting for survival. With them they brought time-worn family bibles containing handwritten birth records and dog-eared pages. One of them was carried by Uncle Isaac. He preached against alcohol, rock'n'roll, dancing, movies, and the Catholics as he pounded the pulpit and the altar, vehemently spewing scriptures and stories he had committed to memory from hearing others preach from a book he'd never read because he couldn't read, his face red, neck veins bulging, and sweat dripping onto his Sunday best white shirt. Unfortunately, these remnants of old-time religion, along with the ignorance and ethnocentricity that were part-and-parcel of it, survived in varying degrees within the next couple of generations in spite of the migration north. Fade's mother Alice was among that progeny. Her romance with a handsome Italian Catholic in Detroit was like the Lord's joke on her southern Baptist family.

*How and why the two of them connected, **collided** would be a better word, has always confounded me. My fondest childhood memory is of times at a neighborhood pub where my dad Salvatore, Sal to family and friends, played accordion with a great-uncle, Dominic, and sang old songs like "Blue Spanish Eyes" and "Goodnight Irene." Mom was none too happy about her son accompanying his dad to a bar, a "beer garden" she called it, and it caused a huge domestic blow-up. Looking back now, I can see clearly that I was a child casualty in a holy war. Little wonder that I consider religion something to be avoided. I'm not sure about a higher power known as God. I don't find the concept of God objectionable, but I can't stomach the judgmental, oppressive Jesus fan club and would venture a guess that **if** God exists, He or She can't, either.*

When I was about ten years old, there was a brief period of time when my father, a non-practicing Catholic, attempted to exert his fatherly influence by taking me to "his" church. Not that he ever went to church regularly himself, but just to "show her there's more than one road to salvation." Catholic church attendance came to an abrupt halt when I began to make observations. A child's eyes and ears would of course notice that the priest repeatedly makes appeals for money to support the parish, a parish of low-income families. A child also isn't reluctant to tell his father that the priest spends more time asking for money than talking about God. The innocent question that left Dad speechless was why the front pews were reserved for VIPs. I remember asking him, "Haven't we given enough money to sit up front?"

As I entered the teen years, my observations continued, along with unwelcome commentary and questions about my mother's religion. "Seems like the Baptists aren't peace-loving people. Your church friends are quick to want the United States to go to war in Iraq, waving the flag and shouting 'Let's go get 'em.' Do they really think God is on any country's side during all the killing?" But the two questions that sent Mom into a tailspin were why there were no Black people at her church and why, if God is about love, the Baptists don't show kindness and tolerance toward gay people, the preacher calling them "an abomination." The greatest affront to dear Mother was my observation about her sister, my Aunt Ellie. "I've heard you say she's a drunk and a fornicator...whatever that means, but I've never heard her say an unkind word about anyone. She's fun-loving and kind. Maybe some booze and fun would be good for your outlook on life."

Emotionally abandoned by his parents, a mother who was out of touch with the playfulness and joy needed by a child and a father who took the path of least resistance by abdicating his parental role, Abe made a decision at an early age to disappear. Detroit is no place for sissies or naïveté, so he got street-smart fast. By the age of fourteen he was experienced beyond his years and able to tough it out through the most dire of circumstances. He recreated himself, adopting a new name without a surname. Even many years later, here amidst the loud surroundings of this huge Gothic nightclub, his adopted home surrounded by kindred souls, he smiles as he thinks how well his chosen name, Fade, describes his escape, reflecting on how he gradually "faded" from the home of his parents. He stayed out later and later each night conducting real-time research on street survival in the most brutal of urban jungles—exploring, interacting, observing, and enduring the punishments meted out by his mother as she prayed for her wayward son's salvation. One night he didn't return home, leaving a bottle of Jameson beside a glass on the kitchen table with a note to his mother:

"Alice, to help you in your search for Wonderland, a place where right and wrong are not so clear and where judgment is subject to ever-changing circumstances. It might be closer to God and reality than the place where you now live."

I'm still awe-struck at the insights of children and young adults. They have a pure and simple way of looking at situations and people...seeing through hypocrisy and injustice that are too readily accepted by adults.

Over the years, Fade honed strategies for survival. He began as a runner, delivering small amounts of marijuana, later graduating to cocaine and making a subsistence living. By the age of sixteen, he had mastered life on the streets and was constructing a life for himself in some of the most blight-stricken, treacherous areas of the Motor City. He found a wealth of resources amidst the urban decay. Public places provide many benefits for the mind and body— the community gym where Fade sparred to sharpen boxing skills and worked out with weights, the public library where he read everything from poetry to history to philosophy, and the Detroit Institute of Arts, a serene place where he learned to appreciate fine and elevating artistry. It was in his favorite library at Gratiot Avenue and Library Street that Fade began a journal, his memoirs, keeping the document tucked away with his song lyrics, essays, and poetry in the loft of the abandoned building where he lives...until a nocturnal existence became necessary. Now his writing is done only where he lives with occasional daylight visits to the library for reading materials.

He is considering whether to make his work available to an underground niche audience and is researching potential publication avenues. Not that it matters much, but it has occurred to him that his writing will be his only lasting contribution and legacy.

Detroit's urban wasteland is littered with abandoned buildings, discarded real estate that is free for the taking like the loft where Fade lives with his muse, the Black Rabbit, and Vader, the beloved pit bull he found in an alley near his building. Music, food for his soul, is also provided free of charge in the city including events like the Detroit Montreux Jazz Festival and concerts at Hart Plaza. One needs only to sit outside the doors of a Black church to enjoy some of the best vocals ever heard. He enjoys performing hard rock, and with a few Detroit musicians, formed a Goth-Glam-Industrial band, Slave to the Beautiful. He had to give it up when he and his friends began their current survival enterprise, one that requires stealth and existence off the radar. Fade also likes to croon Sinatra and Bennett tunes. He would do well on stage anywhere, having inherited a smooth, melodic voice and handsome Mediterranean looks from his father as well as the love of music that is common to Italians.

Fade is a natural leader with magnetic charm. He knows how to get what he needs and isn't above brutal survival-of-the-fittest tactics in situations where the choice is between him and his comrades and someone else. The contradiction, if it is that, is that he also has a strong sense of social justice and charity. Whenever he can, he shares what he has with those in need without judgment about them or their circumstances. He never passes a homeless person without digging into his pocket for a few dollars, responding to those who tell him the money will probably be spent on booze or drugs by saying. "I don't care. Let him get whatever he needs to get through the day." His approach to survival is akin to the great cats such as lions and tigers. He believes they're more virtuous and more perfect than mankind. Mercy and live-and-let-live are preferable, but the lion shows no mercy when threatened or hungry, nor does it feel any guilt about killing to survive. This principle is applied by Fade, now 38 years of age, who has gathered about him a small cadre of trusted "freaks" from Detroit's Gothic nightclub scene and come up with a scheme for making a living, scraping the flesh off the gritty underbelly of the city. They work at night, raiding crack houses, killing the inhabitants, and lifting all the drugs, money, and weapons. Fade is the strategist and tactician, leading by strength of personality as well as the respect and admiration he has earned from the members of his small group, just as he is respected and admired within the Goth community.

Fade's internal reflections on his childhood and self-created life are brought to an abrupt halt by the lyrics of a Siouxsie and the Banshees song booming throughout the cavernous room inside [1]City Club, describing a recurrent dark premonition. "One more kiss before we die. Face to face and dream of flying…. Wind in wings, two angels falling." His thoughts turn to Niv….

She's brilliant and intuitive. She can never be allowed an inside look at my work life. It's bad enough that she recently divorced a ruthless city cop. That fact places both of us at risk. My worst fear is that her ex will discover where I live. My non-identity would be cracked. It's probably time to break it off with Niv. The relationship is intruding into hidden spaces, threatening my survival and continued freedom. So it goes with women. I avoid personal intimacy and long-term commitment in order to maintain secrecy about my work and stay out of the crosshairs of the law, but it's more difficult with Niv than it has ever been with others. It's as if she and

I have been connected for a very, very long time...even before I can remember. My intuition kicked in the first time we met, along with a vague recall of a distant past with her—or was it just drug-induced thoughts? And there's a recurring dream, so erotic and vivid, of the two of us making love in the moonlight in a beautiful rock canyon, both of us sensing that our moments together are numbered. It seems the canyon is in a faraway time and place, but the surroundings are familiar and so real, fireflies, the clearest moonlit sky I've ever seen, the sounds of crickets and night creatures, water trickling through rocks as it has for millennia. This unexplainable familiarity was one of the things that drew me to her, not to mention her intelligence, her selflessness, and her way of simply knowing human nature and life...and unexplainably knowing me. Truth is, Fade, you might not be in control of this relationship.

The night is young at ¹City Club. As if his thoughts are brought to life, Fade catches a glimpse of Niv on the dance floor, wandering beneath the strobe lights amidst flailing arms and Goth bodies gyrating in rhythmic motion. She's looking for him. She looks great, shoulder length jet black hair with straight, Cleopatra-ish bangs, the top pulled up and held in place with her own handmade red leather strips decorated with small smiling skulls, a matching bracelet, a short skirt of Black Watch plaid, tight-fitting corset, black fishnet stockings, and high-heeled knee-high boots. Her makeup is flawless. Fade has learned everything he knows about makeup and hair color from his girlfriends over the years, androgyny being a Goth style that accentuates the feminine side of men, making manly men more attractive. He enjoys artfully applied makeup and wears a red streak in his long black hair at the left front, presenting an entire package in Goth attire that accentuates his Anglo-Italian looks. He approaches Niv and offers her a clove cigarette.

They head toward the club's bar area for Wrong Islands (City Club insiders' twist on the strong Long Islands served here), heads turning as Goth royalty passes.

⁂

[2]Fade lifts Niv's limp body and carries her to the bathroom in his loft to wash the blood from her face and hair. It's caked and will require running water so he lifts her into the shower. He bathes her, dresses her in his pajama bottoms, the ones she likes to wear, and a T-shirt, and gently places her on his bed. Despite their efforts to slip unseen out of [1]City Club and use a circuitous route to his loft, he and Niv had been followed. Fade hears himself sobbing as if he's observing from somewhere outside himself, mind and heart sorrow-stricken, recalling the sound of breaking glass on the roof, his dog Vader running up the stairs barking and growling at the intruders, hearing a gunshot and Vader's yelp, and then everything going black. The bullet penetrated his scalp, grazing his skull and knocking him unconscious in a pool of blood before continuing on its trajectory. The cops left him for dead before turning their attention to Niv, the woman who had spurned a jealous, abusive husband.

There are only a couple of hours left before dawn. My head is exploding and my scalp is still bleeding, but I've got work to do tonight. I'll need the help of my friends. I won't let those scumbag cops get away with what they've done. They killed Niv and Vader. I might deserve death for many things I've done, but neither one of them did. The Lincoln Bar...those fuckers will be there.

Fade finds his phone. "Spam, it's me. You have to come over now. I'll explain when you get here. Pick up John and Keith. Just do it! Bring your guns and be quick. We don't have much time.

I've been shot." They arrive in about thirty minutes. Fade feels a pang of guilt as they climb into Spam's car and speed toward the Lincoln Bar on the southwest side of the city.

I'm selfishly and foolishly dragging my friends into a potentially lethal situation, using them under circumstances that can only elicit their sympathy. You selfish fucker, Fade, these are dirty cops! This vendetta could end all our lives. Fear is palpable in the car…except from John. He's always down for anything and he's more fucking insane than I've ever been.

~~~

Niv's ex-husband and his circle of criminal cops aren't the only ones inside the Lincoln Bar. The place is occupied by numerous badge-holding miscreants, and bloody carnage ensues. After seeing his small band of Goths go down in gunfire, one mortally wounded survivor exits the Lincoln just before sunrise—without Spam, John, and Keith.

I must get home quickly. I'm dying. I have to make it up the stairs into my loft. The Black Rabbit needs to be set free before I pass out never to awaken. I need to finish the writing…

~~~

I've somehow driven home, but I don't remember driving or where I parked. I must have been jarred awake when the car, Spam's car, struck something…like a wall or waste bin in front of or behind the building. I've crawled up the stairs again, for the last time I think, leaving a trail of blood as I've done in the past, but this time coughing it up as I crawl and climb. I'm having trouble breathing. Don't pass out yet…. The Black Rabbit must go free.

I hear a voice. It's distant.

"Abe"

It's getting louder...closer...clearer.

"Abe"

He's calling me now.

"Abe...Abe...You know me, don't you?"

Abe? Abe. That was my name once, long ago when I was a child.

"You've been feeling tired lately, haven't you? I have need of you. If you're ready, come with me now. No more pain. No more worries. No more struggle."

I gain my feet and somehow manage to make it to the bedroom where Niv lies motionless on my bed.

The Black Rabbit is staring at me with those unblinking eyes. He sees through me, doesn't he? He knows everything. He is God. He is Death. He's calling me and I must go. I open the cage door and he sits there, still staring, but he's free now...and so am I.

I move toward the bed and lie down beside Niv.

She looks so comfortable and peaceful.

I reach for the CD player on the night stand near the bed. Catherine Wheel starts to play softly. "Your skin is black metallic," he sings.

I can't lie down and sleep yet, but I'm so tired.... Can't pass out yet. I need the journal.... It's close by. I need to finish my memoirs before consciousness fades. I must finish this. I think I've already been writing all of this down for a while now. I can't remember. I hope I spell correctly. I'm having trouble writing. I just need to sleep beside Niv now...or wake up from this horrible, insane dream with her.

I'm lying down now...so tired.

For the first time in my life I feel happy.

For the first time in my life I feel loved.

For the first time in my life I feel truly free.
For...th...first...time in my li...I feeel...pe...ace...fu...l
I ne...ed to...sle...ep
[3]It must be...a dream... Chanting...monks.
I know them...heir haunting refrain! Distant...familiar...
And closer...much closer...the journal...
All my writing...I leave for...an artist...a kindred soul...to find
Did I write...down...did I finish...that... I...died.

THREE

Spring 2010
Detroit, Michigan

Old World Allure

NIV FEELS THE NEED TO BEGIN anew even though her past, especially the indelible, soul-deep connection with Fade, will remain with her for the rest of her life. She needs to find a place where she can live day-to-day without visual cues tugging at her heart and making her yearn deeply for circumstances that will never be again, not in this lifetime. There must be a place for her somewhere, a place without the ever-present Detroit streetscapes that remind her of life when Fade was present. It probably hasn't helped her emotional state that she has continued to volunteer at soup kitchens and homeless shelters, places that trigger memories of the empathy for Detroit's street folk, "the least among us," that she and Fade shared.

Niv has felt drawn to Italy ever since living in Florence in her early 20s to study art, so she begins to research medieval Tuscan towns. A region known as *Lunigiana*, Land of the Moon, captures her interest and titillates her artistic whimsy. It is described

15

as a magical place, a place of legend and pre-history. Perfect. The medieval [1]*paese* of Pontremoli on the ancient [2]Via Romea, trekked by early Christian pilgrims en route to Rome, beckons. Even though Italian is not one of the languages she has learned, her natural abilities in linguistics will hopefully allow her to earn a living wage in Italy. She contacts the Consulate of Italy in Detroit and begins the application process for a work visa.

FOUR

30 July 2010
Pontremoli, Italy

Straddling Two Worlds

T HE LAST COUPLE OF MONTHS in Pontremoli have given Niv time to contemplate the sighting of the guy who resembles Fade. She has concluded that the vision and her emotional response to it were caused by the hot sun in the piazza, compounded by sleep deprivation during the long flight to arrive at a place where there's a six-hour time difference, followed by several nights of thrashing about in a twin-sized bed in the small quarters she has rented on the third floor of a 15th century building on Via Cavour. Her job teaching English is going well so far, but she has to work very hard at communicating in her not-so-good Italian for every need—transportation, food, directions. The unsettling illusion in Piazza della Repubblica must have been prompted by relocation stress and exhaustion. The Fade look-alike sighting underscores the fact that his presence continues to be strong within her...a comforting presence in this place that is so far from the streets of Detroit, her home.

She was told that Fade and his friends killed every one of the cops in the Lincoln Bar, known to be a rogue cop hangout on Detroit's southwest side. What a great service to the city. She recalls her long, painful recovery from the near fatal assault by her ex-husband and his buddies at Fade's loft. She awoke on his bed to find him lying cold and unresponsive beside her, hearing Catherine Wheel playing, "Your skin is black metallic." The Black Rabbit was gone, cage door open. She vaguely remembers stumbling and crawling down the fire escape stairway to the first floor and faltering out the back door into daylight in the alley behind the building, lapsing in and out of consciousness, unbearable pain with each movement, her head pounding…the surroundings swirling until she vomited from dizziness. Luck was with her that morning when she was seen by a homeless man who was sleeping in the alley, propped up against a dumpster. The dreadlocked, ragged man waved down a passing police car and stayed with her until an ambulance arrived, whispering to her that Fade had often shared money and food with him. He seemed to know her and understand her relationship with Fade. She never saw him again. The next thing she could recall was waking up in a bed at the trauma center, Detroit Receiving Hospital.

As Niv gradually regained her senses and physical stamina, one of the greatest disappointments she experienced in the healthcare system was that the physicians who cared for her during her long rehabilitation were at a loss when confronted with human despair. Most of them chose to limit their focus to their comfort zone, treating her physical trauma, and she certainly had enough of that to keep the trauma team busy—multiple fractured ribs, a dislocated jaw, a fractured skull, and brain injury. Fortunately, she encountered one caregiver who didn't side-step her despair and spent hours with her, exploring her deep sorrow and her fixation on where Fade had gone after death. **A presence as strong as his, cannot just disappear!** Their discussions included the cycling of souls, the curtain between this plane of existence and another, and how chronological time as we know it might not exist in the other dimension. Niv recalls those conversations as she tries to put the recent sighting of the Fade look-alike into perspective. "Pay attention," she was told. As she ponders the intangibles with emotional dissonance, she mumbles to herself, "Damn, thanks doc."

Can shared consciousness inhabit two mortal bodies during lives that overlap in time? The person I saw in the Piazza della Repubblica was obviously alive during Fade's lifetime. Or is this just an instance of physical look-alikes? If there is some connection with Fade, what would bring that man and me to this place at the same time? Synchronicity...meaningful coincidence? [1]*Quantum entanglement? There's science behind that one. Einstein called it "spooky action at a distance." Perhaps I'm not delusional, but it would be far too simplistic to believe that more than one entangled consciousness could inhabit flesh and blood that resemble each other. On the other hand, there might be some purpose behind it because a person who doesn't resemble Fade wouldn't grab my attention and would go unnoticed. Is that what the doctor meant by pay attention? My sister once saw a man who she swears was our father, years after his death. She said she was sure it was Dad standing in the sun at the edge of the garden he loved, smiling at her as she stood at the kitchen window, and yet his face was not exactly Dad's face. If the man in Pontremoli appears again and I have the opportunity to know him, his uncanny similarity to Fade will have to be deeper than his skin to make me realize, without any doubt, that I was led here by forces beyond my comprehension and that his presence, his being, is somehow entangled with Fade's and mine. I would most likely find that the man I saw has nothing beneath the skin that is similar to Fade. And yet there's this feeling I've had since arriving in Pontremoli, the distinct sense that I've been here before and that I was blown here by a fateful wind. Niv...hopeless romantic, lover of fantasy.*

———

Everyone in Pontremoli will be in costume tonight for *Carnevale*. Curious about the purpose and history of the festival in this medieval town, Niv looks it up on the internet. Like the Venetian festival with its distinctive masks, *Carnevale* is an ancient European folk event, originally a pagan festival until the Catholic Church found it easier to turn it into a religious tradition than to eliminate it. The Latin words *carnem* (meat) *vale* (farewell) translate as "farewell to meat," describing the time of year when people took the last opportunity to eat well before food shortages at the end of winter. It was also a time when gender roles were reversed and social norms were suspended. In the Middle Ages, *Carnevale* lasted almost the entire period between Christmas and the beginning of Lent. As she's thinking how Fade would enjoy this festival and its meaning, Niv comes across the following online:

"Before the Beginning, after the Great War between Heaven and Hell, God created the Earth and gave dominion over it to the crafty ape he called Man. And to each generation was born a Creature of Light and a Creature of Darkness...and great armies clashed by night in the ancient war between good and evil. There was magic then. Nobility...and unimaginable cruelty. And so it was until the day that a false sun exploded over Trinity, and man forever traded away wonder for reason." (Samson, a character in the American HBO fantasy series, *Carnivàle,* created by Daniel Knauf and set in Oklahoma during the Great Depression.)

Wow, Fade would be totally down with that. He loved fantasy novels but kept himself grounded in gray reality...no black and white or good versus evil. He'd separate wonder and reason and wouldn't value much of anything over reason. I can just hear him calling mankind a crafty ape and recounting atrocities that have taken place over millennia. He would say the good versus evil bit is overly simplistic, but he would agree that religions sell magic. He once called organized religion "hocus-pocus that is thrust relentlessly upon the ignorant masses with little basis in reason." Commenting on good and evil, he said, "There's often a blurry border between the two. There are acts that are unquestionably evil, but many 'bad' acts are situational with multiple conflicting perspectives." I can hear him, see him, feel his thoughts. Comfortingly spooky how his thoughts continue to be entwined with mine.

Niv decides to venture out onto the streets of Pontremoli where *Carnevale* is taking place. She tries not to set her expectations too high. Detroit's Leland City Club is, after all, the largest, pre-eminent Goth club in the U.S... infamous. She and Fade achieved nobility status at City Club where everyone dressed to the nines in true Goth fashion. Pontremoli's *Carnevale* promises to be an awesome masquerade, so Niv dresses up in her finest Goth outfit and does her make-up as if she's going to City Club. The process induces waves of emotional distress, and she tells herself this will happen in her life without Fade. Forever the wistful child, an analogy that repeatedly runs through her mind is from the story of Peter Pan, the emptiness he felt after the Darling children left Neverland and he realized that the greatest adventure of his life was over, never to be again. Once-in-a-lifetime is just that. Epic once-in-a-lifetime leaves one with a perpetual emptiness... She must find a way to merely live and breathe. Yearning for what once was can be expected, a constant for the rest of her life.

Satisfied with her Goth persona for the evening, Niv heads toward the Piazza Italia. The music is booming, bass throbbing up through the stone pavement under her feet, strobe lights flashing like electric sabers. A sense of home washes over her as she thinks about her name, Carnival, a dubious gift from her mother who told the story about the circumstances of her conception, an account that she has tried to forget. She quietly laughs as she recalls Fade's reaction to the story. "Too much information," he interrupted before she could finish telling it. She began using the name Niv in junior high school to avoid the teasing about clowns and fat ladies that the name Carnival triggered.

So here I am, Carnival at Carnevale. Corny, but it's as if I belong here.

One of the things Niv noticed soon after she arrived in Pontremoli was its mainstreamed alternative cultures—biker-looking guys, Goth-appearing girls, and those whose gender behaviors don't match their physical anatomy—frequently seen on the streets and in cafes mingling and exchanging warm greetings and hugs with locals Fade would call "norms." In Pontremoli, indeed in Europe, social norms appear more evolved, more accepting of all, than in the United States. There's nothing "subculture" about those who live non-traditional lifestyles here. Niv happily senses their strong presence tonight.

What a relief, another reason for a Goth girl to feel at home. Sure hope they play some good music. I'll need to get over expecting to hear The Cult or Catherine Wheel, but the eclectic mix of American disco, White rap, and 70s funk that this DJ is playing really sucks.

After milling about in the thick crowd for an hour and a half, sipping mixed drinks, it's nearly midnight and the festivities are just getting started. Niv senses that someone is looking at her, but that's all it is, just a sense. She shrugs it off and decides to move toward the stage where she can peruse the crowd. Perhaps she'll see some of her students. Kids are still out running helter-skelter across the piazza, dodging in and out of the morass of dancing, costumed people. Children are allowed to stay up late and blow off steam on festival nights. Parents don't seem to feel a need to hover over their children here. There's a strong sense of community and safety. One little boy is throwing confetti at people's faces. A little girl is spraying shaving cream on her dad. He just laughs.

The costumes aren't what Niv expected, nothing like the elaborate, distinctive masks worn at *Carnevale* in Venice. American influence and pop culture are apparent in the Halloween-like costumes and movie characters here—hippies with peace signs and flowers in their hair, Jason Voorhees from *Friday the 13th*, Jack Sparrow from *Pirates of the Caribbean*, and characters from other American films.

So, my Goth appearance isn't as out of step with this event as I thought it might be.

Niv continues to feel a nearby watchful presence. It's not uncomfortable or threatening, but it is palpable.

Here I am, all by myself in a foreign country, and yet I don't feel alone.

Dogs are welcome in public places in Italy including in restaurants. There are many dogs at *Carnevale* tonight, but two large, black German shepherds catch Niv's eye. Then she stops, frozen, when sees him. The shepherds are at his side. Fade's look-alike is here, standing in front of Bar Reno at the edge of the piazza. His hair has been cropped shorter, just above his shoulders. He's wearing black Goth clothing and extreme boots like Fade used to wear! Is this some kind of sick *Carnevale* joke? Even his makeup is Fade-like—gorgeous androgyny.

This is too much, just too fucking much.

She watches in trance-like disbelief as people stop again and again to talk to him. He's obviously well known here. Then he looks directly at her with a vague, familiar half-smile, averting his gaze as he's approached by people who nod, smile, hug him, pat him on the shoulder. Some lightly kiss his cheeks, left and right.

Feeling like she's going to pass out, heart racing, sweaty palms, dry mouth, Niv withdraws through the thick mass of flailing arms and stomping feet toward a line of vendors, hoping to find a place to sit before she falls down. She drops onto a bench where she can still somewhat see him through the crowd.

No, he's not exactly Fade...and yet... Duh! Why not just ask someone who he is? Everyone seems to know him and no one here knows me, so what's the risk? **Just do it.**

"His name is Epifano. He's a musician, songwriter, and poet—Pontremoli's native son. We call him Fano." Niv remains at *Carnevale* for the remainder of the evening, the words of the man in a *Clockwork Orange* costume on a replay loop in her mind. "He's a musician, songwriter, and poet."

Pondering the uncanny similarities between Fade and the man called Fano, she wanders past time-worn doors under glimmering street lamps in a porous haze. It's as if she has stepped back centuries into another dimension inhabited by someone who is warm and kindred but difficult to calculate, like the origin and distance traveled by wind across open water. Ambling Pontremoli's narrow cobblestone [2]*surchetti* (lanes) that veer off

Via Garibaldi, she's bewildered and painfully hopeful. Every few minutes, it occurs to her that she's walking alone after dark on unfamiliar streets in a foreign country. Each time, she tells herself, "Chill already. This is **not** Detroit." The surroundings in the evocative [3]Piagnaro neighborhood are magical and surreal, all passages leading upward to the [4]castle. There is an unmistakable sense of peacefulness and safety here, as if the town and its people are swaddling her.

Then a sudden flashback...Detroit Receiving Hospital... unbearable pain in her head and across her rib cage...unconscious...or was she?

Familiar scenes and people surround me. I'm observer and participant, everything happening at the same time and yet not colliding or competing for time. Mom is here. She's showing me how to make cookie dough. My cat Fizz-gig is here in the kitchen. I'm walking with Fade along Bagley Street toward City Club. We're talking about music. I see the medical team in a small conference room down the hall even though I'm lying in bed surrounded by equipment that beeps and alarms. I can hear them, too. They're saying that I've sustained severe brain trauma. The water of the [5]Magra is crystal clear, flowing briskly over and around the sandstones scattered throughout the stream, gray and white boulders on the banks, as I walk across the old footbridge that connects with Via della Cresa. Spam's mother is crying. The mortuary is packed with his family and friends. My kindergarten teacher, Miss Rafferty, is scolding me for running in the hallway. Tommy McKinney is here, but how can he be? Such a sweet boy. I don't actually see him, but I sense his presence and know he's smiling. I'm swimming in a beautiful slot canyon under brilliant moonlight, and I'm not alone. I've never seen a night sky so clear or stars so bright. Spam, John, and Keith are at Fade's loft. His head is bleeding. I can hear their voices from where I lie in Fade's bed. He tenderly placed me here. He thinks I'm dead. No, Fade, no! Can't you hear me? I'm not dead! A kind fat man in a brown robe speaks solemnly. I can feel his deep sorrow. He says Feo is dead. Feo? There's a police detective at my bedside. He says Fade is dead. A young woman is singing. She's playing a stringed instrument in the doorway of a small church that's surrounded by vineyards near a stone farmhouse. [6]*Teatro della Rosa, the town's iconic cultural center, is small, lovely with red curtains, red seats, and loges along each side. The man on stage...kindred.*

Niv has no idea how long... hours...days...she was suspended in another dimension while she was in the intensive care unit at Detroit Receiving Hospital. Her awakening in ICU was as unwelcome as the mental images that she had experienced were bewildering—the same images and scenes that just revisited her vividly here on the ancient backstreets of Pontremoli, perhaps brought about by the evening's emotions?

Sweet little Tommy McKinney? He died of leukemia when we were in fourth grade. Who is Feo? I felt an uneasy peace and deep sorrow about him. Where is Teatro della Rosa? The woman in the doorway of the church...kindred...seems I should know her. I wanted to reach out and comfort her in her misery. Did I really wake up in ICU? Or am I still dreaming, sleepwalking here this evening? Not so sure I was asleep or dreaming....

Niv stops halfway up the narrow passageway, thinking it would be best to head back to her apartment. She's awe-struck by the cycloramic nature of the recurrent visions in which the past, present, and future are concurrent—a 360-degree, full-color panorama with sound and without a beginning or an end. The cyclorama has repeatedly returned unbidden since that fateful night in Detroit... as it did tonight here on these medieval streets. Oddly comforting, this place and the circular collage of images that she has witnessed once again. She turns back onto Via Garibaldi, heart and mind still reeling from the evening's experiences, and strolls across Piazza del Duomo toward her apartment on Via Cavour. She can't help but think Fano is somehow connected with the surreal cyclorama, but she can't quite reckon it, either... like trying to pin down the origin and distance traveled by wind across open water.

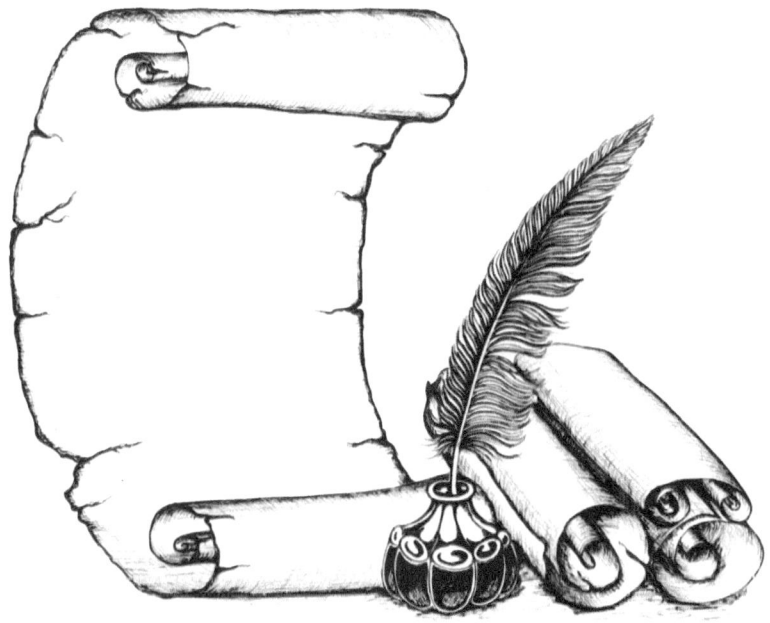

FIVE

February 963 A.D.
Bath Abbey, Bath, England

The Abbess

C YNEWYN ARISES BEFORE DAWN and prepares for her daily routine as Abbess of Bath Abbey. She braids her long auburn hair, wraps it around her head, and fastens it with a cherished antler comb, a gift from her father. She chooses not to wear the elaborately embroidered mantle to cover her head and neck, finding it cumbersome and a garish symbol of her title that she does not wish to convey. An unadorned, undyed wool tunic will do.

This morning Cynewyn's heart and mind are occupied with the greatest happiness she has ever known, albeit a joy that will render her unworthy of the abbess position. The quickening in her lower abdomen has become more frequent over the past couple of weeks. She is certain she is with child. Glorious blessing! However, this blessed event will taint her reputation and cast a dark cloud over Bath Abbey. Her anxiety related to this sobering fact is compounded by awareness of the frequency of death from complications during childbirth. Maternal mortality is so common, in fact, that pregnant women often make arrangements for the care of their other children and maintenance of their households in the event that they do not survive childbirth. Cynewyn fears for the baby and for herself.

God forgive me for my hollow faith, but prayer and poultices are no protection from death for me or my child. In the interest of Bath Abbey and my dear charges, I will hide my condition for as long as possible. The monks will care for me, but this will serve as one more proof of my irreverent, worldly nature and will result in my removal from the esteemed position of abbess. That price and more I will gladly pay for this child.

As a young woman of means, the daughter of a wealthy landowner, Cynewyn was educated at Wareham Nunnery, Dorset. Fortunate to live during the most significant religious and intellectual movement of the Anglo-Saxon period, she is more highly educated than most men, including men within the church. Having mastered Latin, Frankish, and a couple of the Germanic tongues in addition to Old English, she spends countless hours in the abbey's scriptorium transcribing historical documents such as the [1]*Anglo-Saxon Chronicle*, updating the annals of history from the departure of the Romans through the Norman conquest and decades beyond. Cynewyn's literary focus, actually her preference, is secular poetry and literature. Her position and skills grant her latitude to contribute to literary cycles within the [2]*Historia Brittonum*, describing the life of Brutus, founder and first king of Britain, as well as plying creative storytelling in ongoing additions to the legend of King Arthur of Camelot. Cynewyn's proclivity toward Arthurian lore is also inspired by the geographic proximity of Glastonbury Abbey, believed by some to be the burial site of Arthur and Guinevere. The abbess' signature literary style includes historical facts woven into narratives that are written primarily for amusement. Fiction and fantasy bring her pleasure.

Cynewyn's accomplishments, warm personal characteristics, and natural leadership abilities have made her the most qualified person to provide oversight at Bath Abbey. The sanguine, beloved leader has, however, met with disapproval over her opposition to church practices, especially when social justice is lacking, as well as her approach to the reorganization of the abbey. She has proposed that the church not be overly involved in political matters. The conflation of secular and religious matters, in Cynewyn's opinion, creates a sense of quasi-virtuous mission. During earlier times when monastic leaders were under the control of feudal lords, the separation of church and secular concerns might have stood a better chance of acceptance. Since Cluniac reform, however, monastic leaders have been under the direct line of authority of the pope with the intended purpose of decreasing corruption. The abbess has not seen that desired effect, particularly since the beginning of the papacy of [3]John XII, a lecherous and blasphemous despot of the aristocratic Theophylacti family. The irony of her situation crosses her mind, actually more hypocrisy than irony. The same church that abides debauchery and venality in its highest office would not hesitate to strip her of her position if it became known that she is with child. Present personal situation notwithstanding, her ability to garner the support of surrounding feudal lords and promote the good work of the abbey has been negatively impacted by papal bureaucracy.

Cynewyn begins her daily rounds to various locations on abbey grounds where monks are assigned to specialized work. Known for her compassion, her first stop is at the infirmary to visit any ill friars and others from the surrounding area who are in need of care. In Cynewyn fashion, she reminds the infirmarian that ailing monks should not struggle to meet their daily prayer standards. "Do not allow the prayer regimen to interfere with the body's need to rest and recover. I do not believe God wishes constant prayer to deplete energy that is needed for recuperation from illness, just as we would not require the sick to perform physical work, the other Rule of St. Benedict. We must promote physical healing first. They will pray and work when they are able." She often weighs the onerous impact of the monks against their sincere good intentions, holding a personal belief that pathways to salvation are not necessarily mapped through the prescribed religious life. Even though she knows that mortal pitfalls are many and evil exists among mankind, she also believes in the innate goodness of humanity with or without the influence of the church, and she has not observed a positive correlation between church leadership and kindness toward humanity.

It is self-evident that all people need adequate shelter, food, education, and care when they are sick more than they need prayer and sermons extolling the virtues leading to eternal salvation. Salvation is too often presented within the context of what one must do for the church and God—or worse yet what will happen if one does not live a certain way, pray, and tithe...even though most people are poor and downtrodden, merely subsisting. Salvation? How about realism and truth? Give them education and remove the burdens of church tithing! When they are fed and sheltered, only then can they truly focus on God and salvation.

Cynewyn's next visits are to the prior and sub-prior, her delegates if they are needed to travel on church business. They don't know it yet, but she will have need of that kind of support in the near future. Relationships and communication with local and regional church leaders, and more importantly with liege lords, can drastically impact the welfare and operation of the abbey, especially in these days of papal interference. Her subsequent visits are with the cellarer for a report on the food supply at the on-site farm and lastly with the bursar to assess the abbey's financial status. She often allows needy students of [4]ceorl status to be educated at the abbey with their promise of future payment, sometimes foregoing payment altogether, practices that will sooner or later put her at odds with Rome's far-reaching avarice. The abbess reflects on monastery and convent abbeys and their role as academic centers, providing studies in secular as well as religious subjects. Unfortunately, education is only within the reach of the wealthy.

SIX

15 August 963 A.D.
Bath Abbey, Bath, England

Maffeo

*T*HE PAIN IS GONE NOW...MY VISION...FADING. *There's a warm, sticky wetness under my hips. A baby is crying...Elation! My child...my child is born and lives! I must have passed out... for a while...It's getting dark ...blurry images... familiar voices...Please, I beg you...please...take care...of my child.*

"The child is male. The abbess has lost much blood and her breathing is shallow. She is dying. We cannot keep the babe here."

My son...I do not...want to leave you now! So much...to...teach you. Devotion like none I've ever felt...emanating from deep within my soul. Mind and heart...forever intertwined with yours...Why must...I leave you?

Cynewyn hears the solemn voice of the prior praying over her, reciting the commendation of the soul, "To you, oh Lord, we commend the Abbess Cynewyn..." and behind him the crying of her newborn son and the chanting of the monks, her dear charges, becoming more and more distant as her heart slows, the color of her lips fading to gray. Time stands still as Cynewyn passively observes, looking down from just above the small gathering of monks around her bed, still hearing their prayers and chanting...and behind them the cry of her newborn. Benevolent others are present also...just ahead of her, offering help for her passage.... She feels a peace that she's never known, a desire to follow them...a sense of well-being, love, and comfort.

A lone friar sits beneath a starlit sky in the courtyard, overcome by a sorrow that runs deeper than any he has ever known.

My love, my dear Cynewyn, how can I go on without you?

Even through his tears, Ead's grief turns to bittersweet happiness with the realization that the child is born and lives, the son who cannot be claimed as his, and he speaks silently to Cynewyn.

Our son is born under the celestial sign of the lion, one of the four living creatures around the throne of God in Revelation 4:7. He is also born on the day corresponding with the fourth day of creation when the sun, moon, planets, and stars gave physical and spiritual light to the earth. Oh, Cynewyn, how fitting that this child is born under such auspicious signs. Like you, he will possess the cursed blessings of intellect and reason that will lead him to question blind faith and to champion justice as his mother has so righteously and courageously done. How I wish you could know him! How I wish I could raise him as ours! He will indeed be a great man.

The body of the beloved and renowned Cynewyn is prepared for a funeral befitting the Abbess of Bath Abbey. The unnamed newborn is taken to the Benedictine friars at Glastonbury Abbey who are sworn to keep the circumstance of his birth a secret, thereby protecting the legacy of the revered Cynewyn and ensuring Bath Abbey's potential to attract the purses of pilgrims to the burial site of its saintly abbess. Her body is entombed in a prominent crypt in the wall of the church.

⁓

The monks at Glastonbury Abbey name the child Maffeo, gift of God. They call him Feo.

SEVEN

February 990 A.D.
Glastonbury Abbey,
Somerset, England

The Archbishop's Summons

Aaaa MESSAGE BEARING THE SEAL of the Archbishop of
Canterbury arrives late in the afternoon as Feo is finish-
ing his day's work. [1]Sigeric, the newly appointed archbishop, requests assistance with a pilgrimage to Rome where he
will be consecrated and will receive from [2]Pope John XV a pallium, an ecclesiastical vestment. The vestment is the symbol of
authority over the Church of England delegated to Sigeric by the
[3]Holy See. Feo drops the parchment onto the table where he's
working on a music composition, a lute piece for spring liturgy.

*Of course, Sigeric would ask this. He has looked to me and others at
Glastonbury Abbey for support and guidance in the past, having trust in
those who were present during his years here. As always, the abbot, who is
now the archbishop, will receive what he asks.*

Feo walks briskly toward the refectory where he shares a
simple communal supper with the monks and then retires early.

Tomorrow he must dispatch a reply to Sigeric and begin preparations for the long journey to the Vatican.

⁓

Feo awakens to a crowing rooster and dawn breaking through the small, high window in his room. He sits on the edge of the cot pondering the request from the former abbot, a joyless, sober man known as Sigeric the Serious who was educated and received holy orders here at Glastonbury Abbey. The journey will take much preparation, navigation of unmarked trails, and months en route to the destination. Mentally calculating the preparatory efforts as well as the hardships to come, Feo shrugs and sighs, "All for a symbolic stole with a few pendants." Moving to the small desk in his quarters, he dips a quill and pens a response to Sigeric.

To the Venerable Sigeric, Archbishop of Canterbury

4 February Anno Domini 990

The request from Your Grace for assistance in making the journey from Canterbury to the City of Saint Peter is received. I prepare the course to Rome forthwith and shall accompany your retinue.

It is my intention, with your kind permission, to record the course of our journey, including all ⁴mansios along the way, for the benefit of future ⁵viandanti. My considered advice is that the journey begin post-haste to avoid frigid conditions in the mountains during the homebound journey that could place Your Grace and retinue in peril.

Unless you desire otherwise, I will arrive at Canterbury in early March to discuss the route and make preparations for our departure.

Your most obedient servant,
Maffeo of Glastonbury Abbey

As the letter is dispatched to Canterbury Cathedral, Feo delves into the research and mapping of the upcoming journey.

Over the next few weeks, he charts an imprecise, projected course from Canterbury across the English Channel, through France and Switzerland and southward into Italy, approximating the unmapped route known as the ⁶Via Romea. Several possible routes exist, most of them consisting of unconnected segments of ancient Roman roads with uncertain terrain between them. Each leg of the journey must be chosen with consideration of seasonal weather and prevailing political conditions. The Pilgrim's Way to Rome, also called the *Iter Francorum* (Frankish Route), has been traveled for at least two hundred years, but no document exists that reliably describes it. In Feo fashion, he begins the research using the only document available, the *Itinerarium Sancti Willibaldi* of 725 A.D. a record of the travels of the Bishop of Eichstatt of Bavaria. As expected, it provides merely a general course originating far to the east of England with little detail about conditions that could complicate their passage such as varied trail footings, ⁴*refugios* for food and shelter, tracts of land under the authority of local feudal lords, and sections of road that do not connect directly between regions. The distance is approximately 1,900 kilometers over the Swiss Alps and a portion of the Apennines, the mountain range extending into northern Italy, continuing southward to Rome. Feo's routing is a forecast at best. Careful preparations must be made, recognizing that hardships will be encountered and that re-routing during the journey will be inevitable.

As he walks toward the village for one last evening of drink, jovial interactions, and the company of women before the long journey that lies ahead, Feo mulls over the conflicting perspectives that exist between him and Sigeric whom he secretly calls Old Sobersides. Their basic difference is the clash between faith and reason. Feo has long observed the divergence between church dogma, secular philosophy, and reality while he was being raised and educated by the monks at Glastonbury. He has arrived at his own conclusions about religion and the prevailing conditions within the distant Roman Catholic power base. He stifles his opinions, sometimes not as subtly as he ought, and keeps his own counsel as he loyally serves those who raised him and provided the environment where he could study and develop the broad skills he now possesses.

It will take great effort and much patience to ensure that Old Sobersides actually grasps the earthly perils that will be encountered on our journey. Faith and prayer alone will not ensure safe passage to Rome to claim the coveted pallium. How can one who is venerated as a humble servant of God succumb to such hunger for recognition, food for the ego? It is at times like this that I am most cynical about the religious, not only because of Sigeric's feigned humility in this quest...even though he will ride to the door of the Vatican on a donkey to maintain his reputation as a humble servant of God...but also because he has demonstrated time and again his lack of grounding in the real world, refusal to acknowledge its dangers, and silence about the conditions underlying human suffering. Pray, pray, pray while the poor around you are starving and dying. God, if one exists, has blessed Sigeric by placing him a great distance from Rome and the papal archfiends who inhabit it. They would rip out and devour his faithful heart and wipe their bloody mouths on his simple twill cloak. Feo, secure your thoughts and mind your expressions. Purpose, purpose. Safe journey to Rome for Sigeric and his retinue!

Orphaned at birth and raised by the Benedictine monks at Glastonbury Abbey, Feo astonishingly possesses not a shred of religious conviction to the disappointment of the benefactors who coexist with him. Abbots and monks recognize and tap into his natural gifts in languages, writing, music, philosophy, and cartography. His music compositions are heavenly, so good that he has created Gregorian chants for special occasions at the Cathedral of Canterbury. He is even allowed to play his compositions on [7]lute and [8]gittern during ceremonies at Glastonbury, an unconventional departure from church tradition. The religious brothers have resigned themselves to the handsome Feo's secular proclivities, recognizing that his invaluable skills, not to mention his intuition and insights about humankind, are tools more valuable to the church than his worldly ways are worrisome. In spite of his relative youth and his reputation as a wayward soul, abbots and bishops seek his counsel regarding political and strategic matters in times of crisis at Glastonbury Abbey and in regions beyond, especially when powerful forces pose a threat. Feo is adept at discerning covert motives, reading personalities, predicting their actions, and applying dialectic skillfully with charisma—uncommon skills for men of the holy order. Feo's lack of a formal title is more than counterbalanced by his natural alpha bearing, his engaging presence, and his reputation.

The dark, handsome Feo enters the raucous tavern, greeted loudly and warmly by men and women alike. He is well known here and beloved for the earthy traits that are eschewed by the monks. Men are drawn to his masculinity, intellect, and good humor. Women are drawn to those traits, also—but even more so to his exquisite handsomeness. As he strides through the door, he reaches for a [8]gittern that's hanging on a low rafter as if it's kept there just for him. He begins to play a lively tune as the barkeep serves him a tankard of ale. A buxom, red-haired woman smiles and brazenly places her hand on his thigh.

EIGHT

3 - 24 March 990 A.D.
Canterbury, England

Delicate Strategies

C ANTERBURY CATHEDRAL, SEAT of the Church of England and domicile of its titular head, the Archbishop
of Canterbury, looms on a twilight horizon as Feo
approaches the town.

*That imposing edifice is evidence of the extreme lengths to which the church
will go to pay homage to a god who espouses charity. Charity walks a one-way
path in the direction of the church, a thoroughfare with deep ruts worn by the
feet of the poor. The church's expectation of tithing by those who have little is a
hardship exceeded only by the taxes imposed on them by powerful liege lords. It
goads me to observe bare subsistence resources being collected and invested such
as here at this religious estate surrounded by great human need. Ah, but then
there's Saint Peter's Basilica in Rome, built of pilfered marble and occupied
by corrupt hedonists, bearing the façade of a holy place as it hovers over the
struggling masses. Tread carefully, Feo, tread lightly.*

In the shadow of the iconic cathedral, Feo enters the [1]dorter
where a sleeping room has been prepared for him. In spite of
his hunger, he dispassionately partakes of a light supper of dark

rye bread and oat soup with parsnips left for him on a small table beside a straw pallet. As he eats, he reviews his mapping of the long journey across the English Channel and France, traversing a portion of the Swiss Alps and then the Apennines of northern Italy, heading southward to Rome. Alternative routes have been included in his planning. The itinerary must be adaptable to allow for unexpected trackway, weather, and political conditions along the way. Feo is keenly aware that all routes are tentative and that detours are inevitable.

Even though Old Sobersides has a reputation for humility dating back to his early days at Glastonbury Abbey, recognition by the Holy See can make one's sense of authority—and one's head—swell with self-righteousness. Sigeric may have become more commanding since his appointment to Archbishop of Canterbury. If living amidst religious adherents has taught me anything, it is how to divert priorities and intentions that are at odds with the real world. My most careful planning always includes anticipation of the motives and expectations of the other person. Sigeric will surely expect to visit religious sites along the way. He will want to make offerings to memorialize revered servants of God. Ill-advised side trips could endanger the entire retinue and result in a protracted journey. I'll have to steer him toward visits at sites that are safe and not too far off the route to Rome.

The night is short, Feo rising before daybreak to stroll the cathedral grounds and enjoy the sunrise before returning to his room to complete a preliminary list of supplies needed for the journey. Following breakfast in the [2]fraterhouse, he proceeds to the [3]locutory where Sigeric the Serious, hands clasped behind his back, is standing near a glazed window looking directly into it as if he can see through it, obviously deep in thought.

"Good morning, Your Grace," Feo greets Sigeric in formal fashion, hoping for some indication of the new archbishop's mood and current state of humility. He has aged somewhat since

Feo last saw him at Glastonbury. His countenance is as solemn as ever…possibly veiling the self-importance of an evolving church noble?

I hope not. Dealing with an archbishop's naïveté and blindness to worldly realities can be challenging enough, but arrogance, if that trait now exists in the mind of Sigeric, will make this journey difficult and unpleasant.

"I trust your journey from Glastonbury Abbey was a pleasant one, my son. It is good to see you. I am looking forward to hearing your plans for the journey to Rome." So far there is no indication of any change in Sigeric's former demeanor.

As Feo places a wide parchment on the table in the center of the room, he prefaces the upcoming conversation. "As you are undoubtedly aware, there is sparse documentation of routes previously taken. I had hoped there would be some semblance of a traceable route within the [4]*Itinerarium Sancti Willibaldi* which is, as you know, more than two centuries old, but found few useful details within it. Others who have made the journey have provided oral summaries of various routes taken by pilgrims, each one having its own set of trackway conditions, potential barriers, hardships, and risks. I have attempted to map out the safest and shortest routes to and from Rome, realizing that we will encounter places and situations that will necessitate detours for the protection of our pockets and our throats."

Sigeric's face remains expressionless. Classic Sobersides. As anticipated, he proposes, "The honoring of several venerable servants during our sojourn would please God and the church. I would expect to deliver to the Vatican [5]relics from those sites as symbols of my reverence."

*Of course, as expected. Patience! Ply the power of "yes." Voice an affirmative response and **then** diplomatically set limits on Sigeric's desire to demonstrate his piety . . . driven by an underlying motive to impress the pope.*

"Yes, Your Grace. I anticipated that you would desire to pay homage to local saints. It will be done as we are able to do so safely, keeping in mind that some sites are far removed from our route and would prolong the journey. We must avoid delays that will cause us to be caught in wintery conditions in and around mountainous areas if our return takes place in the autumn. Religious sites are also well known to bandits who watch for vulnerable pilgrims carrying donations to pay for [5]relics, not to mention additional toll collection by liege lords if we travel off our route. Tolls will be collected on planned trackways near and across boundaries between [6]curtes, anyway. Our pockets could be emptied by thieves and local tolls long before we arrive in Rome. I will do my best to accommodate visits to as many religious sites as possible."

Sigeric responds without hesitation, his expression somewhat sterner. "Your navigation skills are, of course, the reason I have asked you to join my retinue. However, the Lord guides my journey above and beyond all earthly influences."

[7]*By God's bones! There it is—an edict from His Grace, the Archbishop of Canterbury! As I feared, the humble abbot has been seduced by his expanded scope of authority. His words are those of an autocrat, worse yet a mollifying autocrat who hides behind the cloak of religious piety. "Earthly influences"? Those can kill you and your entire retinue, Archbishop! I can and must play this game in a way that maneuvers around Old Sobersides without openly resisting or challenging him.*

"Yes. There are numerous sites that might be visited. Let us discuss the mapped routes and locations of [8]*refugios* between here and Rome. Perhaps then it will be clear which holy sites will be tractable."

Feo rolls out the parchment on the table. "There is no need to review the better known roads between here and the English

Channel where we will cross by ferry to [9]Sumeran. The journey has along its trackways, many of which were Roman roads, known stops that will allow travelers respite, [8]*refugios* where we may sleep more comfortably than the places where we will otherwise spend nights near the open road. Some *refugios* will also provide us with meals of fresh food. I plan to make frequent scouting expeditions, going ahead of the group to examine road conditions and discern potential dangers including threats to our purse. In this way, we can make informed judgments about whether to pursue a local trackway as opposed to an alternate route and whether to venture to a desired religious site. We will try to avoid any prevailing conditions that would place Your Grace and those who accompany you in harm's way."

So far, so good. Stop here to look for any sign that Sigeric's priorities are even remotely realistic…Sigeric the Serious…No indication.

Following a pause, Feo continues. "The journey from here to the Vatican, including potential detours and delays due to weather, unfavorable road conditions, and other unforeseen circumstances, will take roughly 124 days and 133 days for the return. Much of the road is steep mule track, sections of it seldom traveled and potentially impassable. Portions of the route cross lands controlled by local nobles who will lighten our [10]scrip to collect tolls. When necessary, we will divert, skirting around heavy tax towns and land barons as well as areas infested with roadway brigands. The overall route, therefore, cannot be considered a continuous roadway but rather a series of local trails, loosely connected if at all, where farmers may have tilled the soil creating tedious treading for man and mule. Prudent planning necessitates the allowance of one-third additional days on the way to Rome and two-fifths additional days for the return trip during which we could encounter early cold and snow beginning in the north of Italy. I propose that we depart Canterbury on 24 March with an estimated arrival in Rome of 2 August. Because we will want to avoid wintery conditions in the Apennine Mountain Range and the Swiss Alps in autumn, we should leave Rome by 18 August at the latest—or remain there until next spring. The mid-August departure would allow our homecoming on or around 29 December."

"Remaining in the City of Saint Peter until next spring would, of course, be out of the question as it would delay the important work to be done here at Canterbury," Sigeric laments, disappointment in his voice.

So noted! It remains to be seen whether Sigeric's tune will change when pressure to return to Canterbury this year runs headlong into his desire to visit religious sites in order to be seen as a pious servant of God who is about to receive the pallium of the Archbishop of Canterbury.

Feo draws Sigeric's attention back to the parchment cartograph showing [11]80 stages, places where pilgrims might find respite for at least a night before continuing toward Rome, beginning at Sumeran after the English Channel has been crossed by ferry. As he visually appraises the proposed route, leaning over the detailed map with hands clasped at his back, Sigeric is reminded of the blessing the church has in this brilliant young man, in spite of his infamous worldliness. He recalls the highly guarded circumstances of Feo's birth, known only to the most senior religious leaders at Glastonbury Abbey where he began as monk. He is also aware that Feo was not told of the circumstances surrounding his birth. Sigeric is certain that Cynewyn, the learned and beloved, however unchaste, Abbess of Bath Abbey, would have good reason to be proud of Feo as well as reason to fear for him because of his irreverent nature. The archbishop peruses the stages on the itinerary, unsure whether the distance to some desired sites of saintly persons will allow off-track visits to honor them and buttress his reputation as a reverent and holy man. He is pleased that Feo has planned ample time for the journey.

⁓

The next two weeks are spent in preparation. Feo visits various locations on cathedral grounds to ensure that pack animals, food, and other supplies are available in ample amounts and being readied for departure. His first visit is to the stables. The number of donkeys needed to carry supplies is greater than the number currently stabled. Arrangements are made for four more pack animals to be obtained from neighboring farms. Feo makes a visit to the [12]almoner to apprise him of the projected amounts of money and food that will be needed for Sigeric's journey to Rome. The next day, he enters the underground cellarium to check the availability of meat and staples, realizing that the increased demand brought about by the journey will create shortages for residents, especially now during March when winter supplies have been depleted. Feo expects to hunt fresh meat along the route but will request that a moderate supply of jarred [13]confit, smoked and salted meats, as well as dried quince and beans, be allotted for the trip. By week's end, he makes his final preparatory visit, this one to the [14]buttery where, with the assistance of the monk who keeps it, an estimate is made of the amount of wine and ale that can be afforded this pilgrimage.

⁓

Diggory looks up from his work table as a tall, handsome man knocks and enters wearing a linen shirt under a belted knee-length woolen tunic, neck and sides open. A sheathed knife hangs from a belt around his slim waist. His looks and bearing are unmistakable. His arrival at Canterbury has created much chatter among all who reside here. Diggory grins wistfully, hoping for good will and providence as Feo navigates the upcoming journey.

Saints be praised! At long last I meet the renowned Feo of Glastonbury Abbey, the beloved musician and trusted counselor—the infamous agnostic! It remains to be seen whether his reputation holds true to reality. Obedient servant of God and son of the church am I, but still I admire his cheeky bearing and intrepid spirit. If he is truly as they say, he will counter-balance Sigeric's unearthly ideals with a measure of reason when reason should prevail in the face of earthly realities.

"Good morning, Diggory. I trust my unannounced visit to your workshop is not untimely."

"Not at all. I have been expecting you. Your presence at Canterbury is observed with great interest by all. Preparations for His Grace's auspicious and consequential exodus to the City of Saint Peter are of utmost importance." Diggory's sarcasm is thinly veiled, his tone and devilish grin belying his underlying opinion.

Feo immediately senses the warm, jocular nature of the rotund monk who has been described as "the fat friar who wields weaponry." Diggory is first and foremost, however, a masterful linguist and scribe. His unique skill set is the reason Sigeric has chosen him to accompany the retinue. When he was first told of this monk, Feo began to consider the ways in which Diggory's talents would be beneficial, hence this visit during his second week at Canterbury.

Feo replies with a jibe. "Indeed. I've come at the bidding of His Grace to deplete the cellarium and drive the almoner into poverty, but God will be exalted through His humble servant's sanctification at the Vatican."

Diggory's ruddy cheeks are aglow and his ample abdomen jiggles with delight as he chortles, "You, sir, are a blessing indeed!" Feo is pleased to discover that an earthy, cheerful spirit will accompany the retinue.

Breath of fresh air in this purgatory! Diggory will be a pleasant companion, one with great practical utility as well as an insightful and hopefully trustworthy confidant. It is apparent that he has known life outside the religious domain.

The conversation turns to preparations for the journey, Feo asking for Diggory's input on the types of tools and hunting gear that should be taken. He is pleased to learn that the monk uses a longbow, a skill less common than using a spear or sword and a method that allows hunting from a greater distance. Hunting for fresh meat and protection from wild animals, such as packs of wolves, are primary concerns. Feo also is skilled in the use of a longbow. Together they conclude that at least one additional bow will be needed as a back-up. Diggory offers to make it of yew before their departure as well as an ample supply of arrows. The pack animals will carry some javelins, extra knives, a couple of swords, and axes for gathering wood and clearing brush on overgrown roads. They discuss the need to protect Sigeric and his retinue from bandits along the route, including servant militia, renegades who line their own pockets before passing what is left to the magistrates who send them forth to collect tolls from pilgrims and merchants who cross their locales. The two make a list of needed cooking utensils. The smithy is located near Diggory's workshop. He will oversee the making of all items that require the forge.

"As you are the archbishop's scribe," Feo says to the monk, "I have mentioned to him, and shall remind him, that it would be advisable to create an accurate and lasting account of the route for those who will make the journey after us. In mapping it, there appear to be eighty [8]*mansios* that may provide respite between Sumeran and Rome. Would it be agreeable to ask you to document the itinerary as we travel?"

"It would be my pleasure to do something that will be helpful to pilgrims who will follow," Diggory replies. "The skills of a scribe will otherwise be unused until we arrive in Rome. Besides, it will be a welcome elevation of purpose. I most often copy old manuscripts and worse yet, dispatches dictated by overly pious bishops, most recently His Grace, in obsequious language, supplications of humble servants of God on pure and transcendent missions."

Feo makes no attempt to disguise his merriment at the monk's words as he leans backward in his chair, props his feet on the table, and places his hands behind his head. Diggory goes to a cupboard and returns with a ceramic jug of wine and two wooden goblets. The men are readily at ease and familiar. During their second servings of wine, Feo delves into a subject that has been on his mind.

"Those with whom we will travel will, of course, impact the journey in various ways. Do you have knowledge of those who will be going? Which ones might prolong our journey or place the group in danger?"

"Aye," Diggory retorts. "Of the seven, including thee and me, three are of particular concern."

"I surmised as much, but my opinion thus far is based on limited knowledge, so I look to you for confirmation. You know the history and characters of the individuals."

"Depending on the situation at hand, each of the three, in his own way, could compromise the safety and wellbeing of the group. The least of my concern is Ferand, the eldest pilgrim. His age and frailty could slow us down and add to the burdens of the journey. The other two share equal status as greater risks, one because of his arrogance and ambition, the other because of his naïveté and blind faith."

"Is it possible that you refer to Hew of [15]Saint Augustine's Abbey and Sigeric?" Feo queries. Diggory nods in the affirmative, impressed.

Of course. Feo is, after all, the man whose counsel is sought by abbots and bishops when faced with threatening and even delicate political circumstances. He is a masterful observer of human beings and their motives, aptly predicting behaviors and strategizing how to handle them for a desired outcome. Something tells me he is a fearless proponent of justice who is not soft. In critical situations, Feo would probably not hesitate to use ruthless methods and would feel no remorse for doing so. May the saints preserve us—and him. He bestrides two opposing worlds.

"I had hoped you would have a firm grasp of the characters. You do not disappoint," remarks Feo. "We both know that the Abbot Hew lusts after a bishop's [16]mitre. His efforts at self-aggrandizement will be irritating, and he may use cunning and flattery to further his purpose. Hew does not possess the power and authority to directly create the level of difficulty that Sigeric might cause, but my guess is that he is crafty enough to nudge the archbishop's predisposition to holy pursuits, namely toward collection of considerable [5]relics of saints en route to Rome. He might even make sanctimonious entreaties to divide the group and glorify himself. His machinations remain to be seen. Naïve and unworldly Sigeric is giddy with papal attention and approval, although he conceals it with his long-practiced piety and humility. He hopefully will not exert his newly broadened authority to divert our route to far off-track burial sites of exalted ones or perhaps even to control our daily activities in the name of Christian dogma and salvation. His otherworldly guidance might not be in the best interest of travelers on roadways of real stone and dirt."

"You have given this more thought than I imagined," Diggory observes. "Good Lord willing, I shall act in the best interest of the pilgrims from beneath a lowly monk's [17]cowl." Feo senses his sincerity and trustworthiness.

Diggory's years in pastoral service among vassals and slaves have equipped him with a realistic grasp of the world around him. I have great need of him on the journey and at Glastonbury!

March is passing quickly. As night sets in, Diggory carefully reviews the preparations, knowing that some tools and supplies will be impossible to replace on the road. Unable to sleep, he goes into the cathedral and kneels at the altar to pray for safe passage into Rome, asking the Lord to deliver the archbishop and his retinue from the many dangers on the long journey. His prayer is interrupted by a creaking sound coming from the direction of the nave where the door to the stairs is located, connecting the [1]dorter and the church. She emerges, the beautiful dark-eyed, black-haired laundress, slipping silently across the nave, out the door of the cathedral, and onto the deserted steps, disappearing into the fog that engulfs the dirt street. Diggory smiles.

Feo's reputation has merit. Ah, the pleasures of the flesh....

The monk bows his head and continues his prayers, not asking the Lord to forgive the fornicators but rather to protect

Feo during the upcoming pilgrimage and to offer thanks for the beloved apostate's skills and fortitude.

Early in the third week, Feo again meets with Sigeric, this time to review preparations for the journey, further discuss memorial sites that might be visited along the route, and confirm the date of departure.

"Donkeys, food, tools, and other necessities have been made ready, Your Grace. As you are aware, March finds the supplies of food running low. My plan is to hunt along the way for fresh meat. The monk Diggory is quite a marksman with longbow, and I have moderate skill." A mere nod from the expressionless Sobersides.

Feo continues, "As I told you during our first preparatory meeting, I will scout ahead every few days to discern roadway conditions as well as other threats. We will skirt around villages where sickness is present or high tolls are exacted. The unavoidable tolls will be those collected on or near the main trails. I have provided an estimated amount of coin to the Canterbury almoner, and it will have to be hidden from bandits. Money will not be carried all together in the same place. I have requested concealed pockets to be sewn beneath [17]cowls and masked slits on the sides of the water skins. False bottoms have been fitted to the [13]confit jars. Do these preparations so far meet with your approval?"

Sigeric is in awe, however his face remains characteristically without a hint of his thoughts as he gives Feo a slight nod of approval.

This young man is prodigious. It is not often that a child of God is blessed with such varied gifts. Rare is the person even twice his age who has gathered the experience and knowledge he possesses. Wise choice, Archbishop. If any man can lead us through hardships and peril, he is Feo of Glastonbury.

"Maffeo, there are a number of religious sites between here and Rome that would be advantageous to visit. Have you identified them?"

Feo takes a deep breath, hopefully unnoticed, as he gathers his thoughts before speaking.

*"Advantageous." Ugh...that word belies what really drives the archbishop. I must use the power of the word "yes" and **then** name sites that will not veer us too far off course. In order to show my willingness, I will offer a few iconic, accessible stops that Sigeric will surely agree are desirable. Perhaps I will not be perceived as obstructing the archbishop's holy diversions. It is inevitable that I will have to counter some of his demands for sidetrack excursions that could turn into risky misadventures. Begin with "yes" and take the lead on this conversation.*

"Yes. There is a [18]*pieve* near a [19]village in the Apennines in the Taro River Valley. It is where the French Benedictine abbot and bishop, [20]Saint Moderanno of Rennes, lived. Do you know of him?"

"Ah, I have knowledge of Saint Moderanno. He made a pilgrimage to Rome and later became a hermit monk. Excellent choice."

Without any pause that would allow Sigeric to forge into unsafe territory, Feo offers additional pre-calculated sites that will not cause unduly extended excursions off the itinerary. "There are other consecrated sites within a day's travel to and from the route where we might honor saints. The area around Pavia is replete with churches where saints are honored and where relics may be obtained. I speak, of course, of the domiciles of two beloved saints, [21]Augustine, venerable author of rules for life in a religious community, and [22]Damian, proponent of dyothelitism and minister to the poor and the sick. Would those sites meet with your approval?"

Sigeric appears deep in thought as he answers. "Most certainly. Those sites will be visited in homage to those saints and to the glory of God. As we will be traveling southward through Francia where the [23]monastery at Montmajour and the [24]Abbey of Saint Martial are located, visits to those places should most assuredly be on the itinerary. Our Lord would look favorably upon pilgrims who make visits to those revered sites."

[25]*Eala scate! "Look favorably" indeed, but the favor he pursues will not be from the Lord as much as from the papacy, or so he thinks, when the newly appointed Archbishop of Canterbury arrives at the Vatican bearing relics from those consecrated sites. I would wager that John XV and the miscreants who surround him, if they even bother to show up for the bestowal of Sigeric's pallium, will feign holy brotherhood and acknowledge the baubles gathered by the archbishop, but shortly thereafter they will forget his visit to the Vatican. Sigeric is either naïve or chooses to ignore history and the current conditions within the church. It has been less than a century since the infamous [26]Cadaver Synod and not more than a few decades since the [27]Saeculum Obscurum. John XV is of the same ilk. Sigeric's motives are impractical, unreasonable, and dangerous. Speak to him softly but firmly and with conviction.*

Feo reigns in his thoughts as he readies a response, measures his words, and checks his tone. "Your Grace, the current itinerary pursues a necessarily circuitous route, the shortest version of which will require much off-track skirting of mountainous areas and forging of streams with a goal of arrival in and departure from Rome timed so that we have favorable weather. Should prevailing conditions favor us, we will be able to travel a distance of more or less twelve kilometers per day. If cartography serves us, your sense of direction is correct. [23]Montmajour in Arles and [24]Saint Martial's church at Limoges lie to the south between the center of the Frankish Empire and the sovereign Papal Kingdom, however they are both considerably to the west. Visits to those most deserving sites will require extensive re-routing. The journey to Arles alone will take approximately 38 days each way off the current itinerary. Limoges is even farther to the west. Your Grace is undoubtedly aware that Montmajour Abbey is at a high elevation on an island. We will need to leave the pack animals on land and travel lightly, taking a ferry or boats and then ascending by foot. It is likely that any goods we cannot carry will be gone when we return from the island, therefore we must anticipate having to replace them with unknown and perhaps distant access to resources. We will of course visit Limoges first because it is to the north, more distant than Arles from the border of Italy. We will then cross the Rhone River by ferry or boat, keeping in mind that the area is known to be infested with roadway bandits who lie in wait for merchants. I will ask the almoner to increase the amount of your pilgrimage purse and will visit the cellarium to increase our supplies, hoping they can allocate additional food and staples this late in the winter season. The off-track journey is, of course, unmapped. It is inevitable that we will arrive in Rome two months later than planned and will have to remain there until next spring to avoid winter conditions in the mountains during our return, but it can be done.

I will immediately re-route our journey to Rome to include the westward excursion to visit Limoges and Arles." Silence from the expressionless Sigeric.

Move rapidly to final discussion, allowing him to believe that you have readily accommodated his request. If it produces the desired response, you will have avoided debate or argument.

Feo continues as the agreeable aide-de-camp. "That being resolved, if we may return to something I proposed during our first meeting which would not only serve our fellow man but also promote good will with the Holy See. There is no useful written record of routes to Rome. As you may recall, I proposed that our journey be recorded for posterity. Thanks to you, Your Grace, we will be accompanied by a masterful scribe, the monk Diggory, who would be most pleased to assist in that endeavor." Feo notices a faraway look on Sigeric's face, a thin veil revealing internal conflict.

Good! The strategy is working. No lies or exaggerations. No resistance. I have presented the realities of veering off course to Limoges and Arles. He is weighing the benefits against the hardships and costs, especially the huge obstacle—prolongation of the journey—that his quest for impressive souvenirs and embellishment of his already established reputation as a humble servant of God would bring about.

After a pause without a response, Feo again draws the Archbishop's attention to the subject of a [11]recorded itinerary. "Your Grace, I fear that I've exhausted you with much talk about preparations, so just one more subject before I take my leave. Did you hear me say that Diggory is willing to document our route? If that meets with your approval, I'll bid you good day."

Sigeric responds slowly, still deep in thought. "Diggory...a record of our route.... Yes, yes...of course. Good day, Feo."

Feo adds, "Would a departure date of 24 March still be agreeable?"

Staring blankly in the direction of the window, Sigeric replies, "Yes, yes."

Feo turns and walks toward the door. As he opens it, the archbishop laments, "I simply cannot be away from Canterbury until next spring. My flock, my flock.... Let us proceed according to the original itinerary." Feo acknowledges with a nod, exiting into the hallway before he sighs in relief.

Indeed! It is I who am exhausted with many more challenges to come. If only I were at Glastonbury expending my energies on truly noble and worthwhile pursuits—my writing and my music!

Three days prior to departure, Sigeric's retinue gathers in the [28]chapter house to assure the archbishop that each traveler has made the required preparations, the same ones made by all religious pilgrims. The chances of returning are known to be less than favorable. With Sigeric presiding, each person swears that all debts have been paid and asks forgiveness from anyone against whom he may have transgressed. Each one also confirms that he has established a will identifying his heirs, stating the purpose of the journey, naming the places he plans to visit, and projecting the expected date of return. The retinue is reminded that in the event any one of them has not returned by the projected date, unless their death is known to have occurred, one year and one day of additional time will be observed before his property is distributed amongst his heirs.

All kneel as Sigeric prays for God's protection and His blessing on the long and perilous journey to the City of Saint Peter. Feo stands quietly at the back of the room near the doorway.

On 24 March the retinue departs Canterbury led by Sigeric, riding a donkey and holding a [29]crosier.

NINE

May 990 A.D.
On the Via Romea in France

The Apostate and the Monk

HAVING TRAVELED WELL INTO [1]Frankish territory, sweet aromatic bouquets are carried on mild spring breezes. Blooming [2]muguet and primrose adorn the countryside. Accompanied by Diggory, Feo forges ahead of the archbishop to assess conditions along the roadway.

"Good Lord willing, spring's soft arrival portends a pleasant and uneventful summer," Diggory says wistfully as he pauses to take a deep breath and scans the verdant terrain.

"We can only hope, dear Father. But you will also pray, of course." Feo winks and chuckles, assured of the friar's jovial nature. Diggory responds with a deep, gleeful chortle, knowing that Feo's impudent joke is a strength, a refreshing departure from the sober interactions that fill his days at Canterbury. "Aye, believer I am and pray I shall for your irreverent soul," Diggory retorts.

Even before Feo entered the workshop at Canterbury, my life and service outside the monastery had shown me again and again that faith is often at odds with life's realities. Feo's observation that "the religious seek enlightenment and attain blindness" holds more truth than I care to admit. I will, of course, continue to pray, especially for Feo. I fear he will collide with forces that would do him harm.

The past two months have provided many opportunities for deep, intimate conversations between Feo and Diggory away from the retinue, especially during hunting expeditions with longbows and javelins. It was during one of their talks that Diggory shared his personal history. It began when Feo, in jest, mentioned Diggory's ginger hair, prompting the amiable monk to acknowledge his genealogy. He confided that he is the bastard son of a Viking, the product of a raid into the Germanic territory where he was born. Listening intently, Feo smiled and commented that this would explain Diggory's adventurous nature, his fondness for food and drink, and his skill with weaponry. There were moments when they delved into personal experiences, observations, and beliefs, and there were episodes of light-hearted banter. The bond tightened between friar and infidel. Feo once came close to sharing the secret Ead had revealed to him, the truth about his birth, now engraved on his heart and mind. He quickly stifled the temptation. He had come to love Diggory as a father figure, but he never had, and never could, share the identity of his mother and father with anyone.

As they approach the village of [3]Bar, Diggory's deep voice breaks through Feo's introspection. "We need to increase our supply of ground rye if possible, perhaps in the village." On the outskirts of town, a man approaches with cart and mule headed in the opposite direction. Diggory greets him and inquires, "Would you know if there might be any flour for purchase in town?" The bedraggled commuter retorts, "Hah! Chance that you ask about flour! The crops went bad. People in Bar suffer from [4]fits and blackened fingers and toes. I was summoned to bring grain from [5]Breone and did so only to have my purse lightened by the magistrate. He demands a price from all who pass, particularly merchants. The tax he charged left me with precious little. I should have kept the grain!" Feo and Diggory nod, stopping at the side of the road as the man and donkey continue on their way trailed by an empty cart. Feo observes, "He has provided the two answers that we sought. No rye flour and no passage without a price." The need to use unbroken trails to skirt around Bar without supplementing the supply of flour is evident to both men as they turn back toward the roadside camp where they left Sigeric and the others.

Passing a wide creek, Feo pulls out the yew longbow made by Diggory and takes aim at a swan, the largest among a bevy swimming near the bank. There is loud trumpeting, commotion, and flapping of myriad wings as the swan is struck by the arrow, droops to one side in the water, and the bevy takes flight. There will be fresh meat for the evening meal and enough to last for the next few days. Diggory's mouth waters as he wades knee-deep to retrieve the fowl. The travelers will be grateful for something other than the dried legumes and confit they so often must eat.

"Your skill at bow-making be praised, Father," smiles Feo. "The arrow flew swift and sure."

"The skill of the archer be praised, my son." Diggory's eyes twinkle in merriment as he slings the huge bird over his shoulder and they continue to walk back toward the roadside encampment.

Feo reads Diggory's thoughts. "With a bit of luck, we have heard the last of the archbishop's stern guidance on fasting in observance of [6]*quadragesima paschae*. The prolonged duration of self-denial weakens even young, healthy men who are not on a strenuous journey. Scant nourishment does not keep good company with advanced age and the physical demands of the road."

"Aye, to be sure," agrees Diggory. "The elder Ferand is weakened. His one desire is to complete the journey to the City of Saint Peter, and I pray that he will at least arrive there. His stamina has been depleted by the fasting." Never missing an opportunity for humor, even at this own expense, Diggory adds, rubbing his rotund abdomen, "And I would be the last person to be disappointed if fasting disappeared from the liturgical calendar altogether!"

They both laugh until Feo is sobered by thoughts of what is certain to come. "Fasting aside, further clashes of faith and reality are inevitable. If it were just a matter of conflicting ideologies, I could oil my back and let it roll off. The odds are too high, however, during an undertaking such as this arduous journey. We could pay with our lives for the relentless practices of the faithful."

Diggory's enjoyment of Feo's company turns to unease.

Aye, and those devout practices are undergirded by ambition and ulterior motive. We have both observed the Abbot Hew's behavior toward Sigeric and heard his nauseating, obsequious responses to the archbishop's every utterance. Hew has no loyalty except to himself and will stop at nothing to advance his upward creeping. Feo has aptly described him as a spider in a robe. Even though Sigeric's aspirations have been realized and he seeks final confirmation, his naïveté makes him susceptible to the spider's venom.

TEN

19 May 990 A.D.
Bath Abbey, Bath, England

A Father's Heart

NEWS OF SIGERIC'S JOURNEY to Rome to receive his ecclesiastical vestment has reached far and wide, including the role of Feo of Glastonbury Abbey in mapping the route and navigation. The monk Ead feels great pride, and yet his heart is heavy. He did not have an opportunity to bid Feo farewell and safe journey. He weeps softly as his memory transports him to a tender time and a learned a young woman, the revered abbess who possessed the same sense of social justice and voiced the same remonstrations that her son does now, often to her own detriment. Ead agonizes over what might be a wasted destiny for Feo whose gifts are so many. He wonders…

If Cynewyn had lived, to what fateful end would her insights and benefi-cence have led her? And where will they ultimately lead our son? The [1]Saecu-lum Obscurum, the Rule of the Whores, is not long past, and elements of its corruption remain in Rome. While Feo's tendencies toward merriment and pleasures of the flesh might not be considered sins under current papal norms, his opinions about justice and the distribution of wealth, as right and virtuous as they are, would not be well received. Dear Lord, please guide and protect my son Feo on his dangerous sojourn but even more so during his perilous venture into the Vatican among vipers at the behest of the pious and naïve Archbishop Sigeric.

In his early 30s when Feo was born, Ead is now 60 years old and in failing health. His mind travels back several years to a decision made after much prayer—to visit his son. He waited until Feo turned 20 years of age before making the trip to Glastonbury Abbey under the guise of a monk seeking a music composition for mass. Glastonbury, the iconic Benedictine monastery, had provided an environment in which Feo could study, even if the conclusions he reached did not align themselves with the church. He had already gained widespread notoriety as an invaluable musician, counselor, and emissary of the church in spite of his reputation as an apostate known to question church practices and papal motives.

Ead's mind wanders back, reliving his first meeting with Feo in 983. He has indeed inherited his mother's good looks and Ead's dark hair and olive complexion. The young man quickly intuits a deep connection with the visiting monk, and their conversation drifts from a liturgical composition to thoughts on abbey life and the direction of the church. It is apparent to Ead, even during this first meeting, that he should reveal to Feo the story of his birth.

Feo is a man who can handle any truth. Who am I to deny him the truth about his birth that I have kept to myself for so many years? My son, my son…. I know that he will not judge me harshly for loving his mother and longing to know him.

"Feo, your reputation as an [2]apostate, however beloved and respected, one who discerns the injustices within the church and its secular entanglements, reminds me tenderly of the late Abbess of Bath Abbey, Cynewyn. Do you know of her?"

"Yes, of course," Feo replies. "Cynewyn holds saintly status. Many pilgrims visit Bath Abbey to pay her homage. Her legacy is one of kindness and transcendent understanding...a legacy that also serves to fill the coffer of Bath Abbey."

Bittersweet reality flashes through Ead's heart and mind, brought on by Feo's strikingly truthful words.

*Of course, this is **her** son speaking, and he is living up to his reputation!*

Feo immediately realizes that his off-handed remark might have been offensive to this monk from Bath Abbey.

Mind your sharp tongue, Feo, and remember that church benevolence has provided you, an orphan, with sustenance and an education.

Before Feo can soften his commentary, Ead responds, "You describe her reputation well—and the abbey's opportunism in memorializing her goodness. I admire your courage and insights. I have lived as a silent servant of the church who cherishes the memory and influence of Cynewyn. I knew her well and miss her greatly to this day."

Feo's interest is piqued. He senses Ead's deep sorrow and asks the monk to share his memories of the renowned abbess. The next couple of hours are spent in a tender verbal biography of Cynewyn, her impact on the abbey and those around her. Ead's manner of telling this story, his voice and facial expressions when speaking of her, lay bare his devotion to her, not just as the titular head of Bath Abbey but as a woman. Ead's recall includes deep conversations with her about humanity, altruism, and love, his reminiscences providing a less than thin veil over the nature of their relationship. Feo perceives that Ead simply cannot hide what unquestionably was, and remains, a deep love between a man and a woman. In Feo fashion, he probes at the truth. "How did Cynewyn die?"

Ead answers with a look of perpetual grief. "She died in childbirth." Feo's mind begins to race.

There's no need to state the obvious. The abbess was unmarried.

There is silence for a prolonged period of time until Feo, perception afire, states, "And the child was yours."

After another long pause, Ead continues, "It has been the great tragedy of my life that my son, our son, was sent away to protect the legacy of the Abbess Cynewyn and ultimately the good name and assets of Bath Abbey. No one at Bath knows that I am the father of Cynewyn's child, a boy, born on 15 August 963 and raised as an orphan. I have been a coward, but the truth would have cast aspersions in the direction of the abbey and Cynewyn." Feo's head is spinning but he maintains his composure, as always.

15 August 963, the day I was born! I have had this feeling since Ead arrived...that I know him or should know him...somehow. The request for a music composition did not seem like the sole reason for his visit.

"So, there are unexpected truths in life. I only wish I could have known my mother as I shall come to know you, Father."

Now 26 years of age, Feo has evolved into a church asset on a variety of matters, so it is no surprise that the archbishop requested his cartography and navigation skills for the journey to Rome. Ead is sure that Feo has maintained a symbiotic relationship with monks, abbots, and bishops across the region not only because of his valuable skills but also because of their reverence for Glastonbury Abbey, seat of Saint Dunstan's monastic revival in England and the monastery where Sigeric, now the Archbishop of Canterbury, was educated and received his holy orders.

Looking back now on his many visits with Feo over the past seven years, Ead feels a deep, peaceful fulfillment. His health declining to the point that routine daily activities drain his strength, he knows he will never see his son again. Feo is well on his way to Rome, and Ead can only wonder what hardships will be encountered on the long, perilous journey.

Safe journey, Maffeo. So like your mother! I can pass into eternity knowing that our son is a man of great consequence.

ELEVEN

19 May 990 A.D.
¹Great St. Bernard Pass, Swiss Alps

Alpine Perils

SPRING HAS ARRIVED GENTLY in southern Francia where the days are mild and aromatic with the scent of clover, wild sage, and lavender. As the group ascends day by day into the mountains, however, the days have become cold and rainy and the nights frosty, even on the lower climbs such as this alpine meadow where the weary travelers stop earlier than usual to set up camp. The mountain rain has been unforgiving, driving a chill deep into the bones. The cold downpour has subsided, afternoon sunshine breaking through the clouds. The campfire is stoked early in hopes of drying and warming clothing as well as the bones of the pilgrims.

Feo smiles as evening darkness sets in, recalling Diggory's futile fishing attempt at an icy alpine ²tarn while there was still some daylight. Always eager to find fresh meat, the ravenous monk tossed a line and hook into the water amidst remnants of floating ice only to snag a clump of underwater vegetation, losing his balance when he tugged at the line and tumbling head over heels into the frigid water. Returning to camp soaking wet and shivering, mud and moss clinging to his face and neck, the big monk was in an uncharacteristically foul mood. "Perhaps those tenacious underwater roots swallowed up all the fish," Feo goaded him with merriment that quickly spread to the others, no one having the audacity to mention the fact that there are no fish in alpine tarns. No need to further humiliate the disheveled and dripping Diggory who good-heartedly acknowledged the banter as he wrapped himself in a blanket and hung his cassock to dry over a shrub near the campfire.

As they settle in for the evening, Feo's thoughts turn to another incident today that was not as benign and humorous as Diggory's fishing misadventure. Seeing the tender early growth of wild flowers and herbs across the mountainside meadow, one of the travelers had set about gathering whatever might add flavor to the evening meal. The gatherers plucked some fresh green leaves believing they were [3]cow parsley. Fortunately, Diggory recognized the leaves as [4]hemlock, and disaster was averted. Feo's concern is what he observed at dusk.

The stealthy spider Hew must be watched. Why did he return alone to the meadow this evening? He told Sigeric he sought solitude for prayer. He hides something beneath his abbot's robe. His motives are corrupt.

Lying awake under the stars, another tender but troubling thought nags at Feo.

Ead and Cynewyn were star-crossed, and yet they shared a love that does not come along in every lifetime. He loves her as if she still lives, and indeed she does live in his heart and mind. Even I can feel her presence in the gifts my father tells me that she gave to me, cursed gifts that I would not be without but that place me at odds with those who raised me...just as they did my mother. Providence has been in my favor thus far, but the day will come when my sense of justice will collide dangerously with the motives of the ambitious and powerful. Cynewyn died young, and I shall die young. I only hope that I, too, will have one great love in my lifetime. But...could I ever be deeply devoted and true to one woman?

Feo drifts into a sound sleep as wolves howl in the distance, a familiar and expected sound in the wilderness.

Just before dawn, the travelers are awakened by the loud braying and kicking of the donkeys that are tethered to graze near the camp. Running toward the sound, Feo realizes what is happening. A pack of wolves has attacked the donkeys. Diggory is not far behind him. As they approach the donkeys, they discern vague moving figures on top of a donkey, now on the ground. The sickening sound of death—wheezing and the donkey's attempt at braying—as a large wolf applies crushing force with teeth on its windpipe and the others rip fur and flesh. Feo and Diggory read each other's minds as they rush to cut the main tether line and retreat, leading the remaining donkeys away from the gruesome scene at the risk of being attacked themselves. The methodical, rapacious carnivores are totally engrossed in just one kill for the pack. There will be no saving the poor creature that has become prey.

Sunrise finds the group of stunned travelers back on the roadway and descending into Lombardy, minus one donkey. By late morning, a chill remains in the mountain air, even though the travelers are damp with perspiration under a glaring sun.

TWELVE

30 June 990 A.D.
¹Pavia, Italy

Saints and Sacrilege

RUE TO HIS WORD, FEO HAS led Sigeric's retinue a day and a half off the route, arriving in Pavia to pay homage to ²Saint Augustine and ³Saint Damian and purchase memorial relics. The travelers will later spend the night at a campsite beside the roadway not far from town. Bored and irritated with this off-track excursion, Feo strolls the parish grounds, lingering near the back of the church while he waits for the pilgrims who have gone inside.

I would give a king's ransom for a tankard of ale and a romp with a comely woman. Time drags on while I accompany Sigeric on a mission to claim a piece of cloth!

The sound of a woman softly weeping reaches his ears. Feo follows the sobbing to a locked door at the rear of the church. Placing a wooden crate beneath a barred window, he steps up onto it and looks inside. A young nun sits in a sparsely furnished cell holding a newborn, still wet from birth. The afterbirth, covered with flies, is visible on a nearby straw pallet. Feo's thoughts immediately turn to the obvious reason for this nun's imprison-ment…and to his mother and the circumstances of his birth.

Barbaric. She gave birth alone in this dreadful tank. She is being pun-ished for a high transgression—breach of chastity—sequestered until the child is born, followed by excommunication. Fate was kind to Cynewyn, not in dying young but in remaining in her position as Abbess of Bath Abbey. She was spared humiliation and shielded by the monks at Bath Abbey, even though their motives in preserving her virtuous legacy were driven by oppor-tunism and the need to conceal a scandal.

Feo's attention is seized by the rattling of keys and creaking of the cell door. He ducks beneath the window to avoid being seen as a misshapen monk enters. The monk has not aged well, his face deeply furrowed. He is bent at the waist, dragging one foot. His expression bespeaks a vile heart and mind, his mouth forming a dastardly smirk as he limps toward the young nun and her baby.

If it can be believed that the state of one's spirit is manifest in the flesh, before me is proof of it. This elder monk must be one of the church infor-mants, eyes and ears alert for those who transgress against the church's beliefs about sin, especially here within the bastion of [2]Saint Augustine. Discovery of this woman's condition must have given him immense demented pleasure. If I live to be as old as this decrepit troll, I shall never understand the hypocrisy of a church that speaks of a loving God while its agents indulge in this type of cruelty.

The old monk's high-pitched, nasal voice is as grating to the ears as his appearance is repugnant to the eyes. It resonates through the dank cell like a hyena's laugh. "So, the babe has come. Good. Arrangements have been made. Is the child male or female?"

"I beg you," the mother cries, arms wound tightly around her newborn, not answering the monk's question. "If you will just allow me to walk out the door with my baby, it will save you the trouble of dispersing us. We will disappear, never to be seen again. Have mercy!" Her body heaves with each deep sob. The sound of a mother pleading for her child is more than Feo can bear.

What the monk says next prompts Feo to take immediate action. The cruel one pries the mother's arms from around her newborn, removing the crude swaddling to see its gender. "Excellent. She will bring a higher price than a male." As if exhaling his words through mucus, the robed troll emits wheezing nasal sounds as he speaks. He makes no attempt to soften the brutal plan for their fate, but rather enjoys its devastating impact. As the sister continues to plead to be released with her baby, he speaks loudly over her in a raspy sing-song manner. "Allowing an unchaste sister to live in any of the surrounding locales could subject our religious community to disfavor among liege lords who are otherwise generous and cooperative. The slave trade is thriving in Venice, so I have arranged your transport on the morrow. The child will be cared for as an orphan of unknown parentage until she is old enough to be of value. The church ⁴almonry will twice benefit from this disgraceful situation."

Damn this monk! I swear this abominable lecher is a dead man. No knife, no bow. It will appear a natural death.

The monk leaves the musty cell, locking the door behind him and limping slowly toward the ⁵locutory, a building that is separated a good distance from the church across a wide grassy area bordered by beech trees and tall bracken. As a senior church official, he is en route to the welcoming of Sigeric, Archbishop of Canterbury, and his retinue. Feo swings into action.

The ⁶mandrake I've been saving.... He is not worth the waste of valuable elixir, but there is abundant reason to use it to send his ignoble soul crashing ass first into hell.

Slipping quickly into the church, Feo dips the water skin that he wears on his belt into the stoup of holy water, filling it only partially, just enough to dilute a lethal amount of [6]mandrake, before looking in all directions and stepping outside unseen. Proceeding hastily to the outer edge of the wooded area adjacent to the [5]locutory, he retrieves the powdered mandrake root from his pocket and funnels an overly generous amount into the water skin, gently rolling the vessel to mix the deadly potion. He then reclines against a tree, whistling a merry tune as the old monk limps slowly toward the locutory. Hearing Feo's whistling, the evil one turns to face the wooded area and sees a handsome young man, quickly surmising that he accompanies the Archbishop of Canterbury. "Good day, my son," he rasps. "I trust you accompany His Grace the Archbishop."

"Very astute, Father. I am his navigator and ironically one who is in need of directions this day. Might you give them?"

Seizing any opportunity to impress and promote church good will toward pilgrims, especially one of such note as the Archbishop of Canterbury who is en route to the Vatican to receive an ecclesiastical vestment, the old monk slowly hobbles, almost slithers, toward Feo who is feigning a traveler's weariness. "How may I be of service to you and the archbishop?"

"We veered from our route to visit this revered site, and now I fear that my bearings are off. We will need to head south to regain our trackway. Is there a place in that direction that might provide shelter for the night?"

As the monk moves within reach, Feo stands as if to greet him but instead slides one arm around the old man's neck and firmly clasps a hand over his mouth as he pulls him backward into the copse of trees and vines, forcing him to the ground. Sitting on his chest and pinching his nostrils, Feo shoves the water skin's narrow opening into the monk's mouth, squeezing the deadly potion into his throat and glaring into his terror-stricken eyes, forcing him to swallow again and again until the water skin is empty. Then pressing a hand across the monk's mouth, Feo straddles his torso to maintain a firm grip on arms and shoulders until the evil one drifts into oblivion, never again to awaken in this world. As his eyes flutter and he struggles weakly, Feo whispers to him, "You are the servant of Satan if he exists. I regret that wasting precious mandrake on the likes of you will deprive me of several euphoric interludes during my long journey and even more so that it renders such a quick and painless death for you." Unable to resist the temptation to take one last jab at this holy man's hypocrisy, Feo adds, "Benevolent...or rather malevolent...Father, take solace in knowing that consecrated water from the church stoup constitutes your death elixir, ordained by God for this truly just purpose."

As the monk's breathing ceases, Sigeric and his retinue can be seen through branches and bracken making their way toward the [5]locutory across the grassy clearing led by church officials. Remaining hidden, Feo continues to clasp his hand across the mouth of the now motionless creature whose eyes are open, fixed. When the group has entered the locutory and Feo is satisfied that it is safe to emerge, he exits the copse of trees and walks nonchalantly onto the lawn, on a mission to find a place where the old heinous one will be found dead of natural causes.

I will return after dark to move his body. And there's the nun and baby....

Curtains...the blue ones in the small room adjacent to the church nave... those will have to do.

Known to have a routine of late night prayers, it is no surprise when the senior monk is found dead in the small room near the church [7]nave the next morning. Father Agnolo has not been feeling well of late. His faltering health and increasing forgetfulness have been noticed. He probably forgot to lock the cell where Sister Aemilia was being kept. The door and latch are unbroken, and the cell key is with the dead father who lies amidst a jumble of draperies. He appears to have grasped them as he fell to the floor.

With the rising sun, Sigeric and the travelers are awakened in their roadside encampment not far from Pavia by a wailing baby swaddled in gray fabric recognized by Diggory as cloth from a nun's habit. The child is cradled in the arms of a young woman in a makeshift blue dress tied at the waist with what looks like drapery tie-backs. No verbalized questions, no explanations. Feo will provide a story when the subject is broached…and it will be. They continue the journey southward.

THIRTEEN

5 July 990 A.D.
On the Via Romea north of
Pontremoli (Puntremel), Italy

Mystics and Murderers

FTER TRAVELING A HALF DAY'S distance from [1]Sce
Benedicte where the pilgrims passed the night, Feo
leaves the group at a roadside encampment and scouts
ahead on foot. Located on a high valley where the Magra and
Verde Rivers meet in northern [2]Lunigiana, [3]Puntremel is a valuable military and trade stronghold with [4]a battlement overlooking
the routes winding downward from Apennine Mountain passes.
There are two purposes for Feo's scouting expedition: to assess
conditions flanking the mountains where spring run-offs may
have washed out the trailways and to determine whether tributes are being charged for passing through Puntremel. Under
the control of the wealthy and powerful [5]Obertenghi family in
a symbiotic relationship with the Holy Roman Church and its
bishops, Puntremel is prime territory for heavy toll collection.
Of even greater concern is the frequency of conflicts between

powerful factions, making it nearly impossible to know whose territory the road may cross. As he draws near a small settlement not far from Puntremel, he is hoping to find some indication of the area's disposition toward travelers.

The sound of voices becomes more and more distinct as Feo proceeds in the direction of the village. From inside a copse of beech and pine trees, he remains unseen. A ritual is taking place. A wave of nausea washes over him as he recognizes the purpose of the solemn mass at an open grave—the [6]Mass of Separation. A priest throws a handful of dirt over the man who stands upright in a grave, declaring him "dead unto the world but alive unto Christ."

Such ignorant cruelty! If leprosy is God's punishment for what Christians believe is sin, I shall surely die a horrible death.

A young woman lingers as the priest and the few attendees leave the gravesite. The stricken one, now officially dead to society, climbs from the grave wearing the cloak of the leper and a bell to alert people of his whereabouts. He is expected to keep his distance from the community on penalty of death. Apparently unafraid, the woman draws near to speak to him. After a conversation that lasts several minutes, she hands him a pouch and they part ways. The leper walks slowly toward a hilly forested area. She turns toward the village.

What brought her to the graveside for this loathsome mass? The shunned one, poor creature… must be related to her?

Feo continues walking toward [7]Arzengio, a small settlement on the outskirts of [3]Puntremel. The village is close enough to provide information on prevailing conditions around the larger town. He can feel the remnants of the old paved Roman road beneath his feet as he weaves around what remains of a rock boundary wall, noting an ancient pagan sacrificial stone nearby.

Entering the settlement, he scans the sparse number of locals in search of any amiable stranger whom he might ask whether conditions are favorable for travel through Puntremel. As he approaches the intersection of the [8]*cardo* and [9]*decumanus*, the melodic strumming of a [10]psaltery and a woman's voice reach his ears. He follows the sound. At the center of the settlement beneath an [11]architrave bearing the carving of an [12]apotropaic mask to ward off evil sits the same young woman he observed earlier at the gravesite during the ghastly excommunication. Feo listens from just across the thoroughfare. Her voice is mesmerizing, her aura magnetic as she serenades the empty street almost as if she knows he is listening.

> *Blown by fateful winds*
> *Maffeo guides t'ward the Holy See*
> *Your journey mapped with an unseen path*
> *That leads you here to me*
>
> *Just outside* [3]*Puntremel*
> *The Navigator does veer*
> *Leading onward to Rome, Trusted Agnostic*
> *An archbishop's mantle to clear*
>
> *Divert this way,* [13]*Viandante*
> *To a message at two oak trees*
> *Then at the sanctuary at San Cristoforo*
> *Our bond, beyond blood, we shall seize*

As she finishes her song, Feo attempts to gain his composure, having been caught off-guard by the mysterious allure of this woman and the words of her song, words that could not be by mere chance. Her chestnut hair, falling about her shoulders, has golden highlights in the midday sunlight. As he crosses the thoroughfare, her green eyes become piercing, looking straight into his heart and mind from behind liquid pools adorned with long, wispy lashes.

What is this? She's not stunningly beautiful and yet she is a temptress. Even more alluring is her ability to sing of that which she could not know. Is she a witch? If so, I hope she will continue to speak to my heart with soft, enticing magic!

Feo, in spite of his experience as a lover, is shaken by his uncomfortable pleasure in the presence of this young woman. He is reminded of the meaning of the word "moonstruck" as he first speaks to her. "The words of your song and the inscription above your door, [14]*'Ostium non Hostium,'* make me feel at liberty to ask your name."

"Fastrada," she replies, adding nothing more as she attempts to maintain her own composure.

Yes, without a doubt this is he, the one whose arrival was foretold to me. Be still my heart. He is more handsome than I ever imagined.

"You seem to know the nature of my journey without knowing me," Feo probes.

She softly responds, "I have known for some time that you would arrive leading a group of [13]*viandanti* (pedestrian travelers) and a man of the church. Awareness of your coming, without bidding, simply found its way into my mind and my song. Whether you choose to believe this is your choice."

What manner of far-fetched fantasy is she revealing? My mind and heart are reeling from this encounter, beginning at the gravesite on the outskirts of town.

Having long ago grown accustomed to prescient flashes that frightened her during childhood, Fastrada realizes that the man in the song stands before her in the flesh, the prediction of his

arrival handed to her from some unknown source. She is determined to focus on the tangible present and the danger to Feo and
the archbishop's retinue, recalling a conversation she overheard
this day between two of the [15]magistrate's local recruits at the
street market. They had somehow neglected the road through
[16]Passo della Cisa, allowing a group of [17]*pellegrini* (pilgrims) to
arrive at [1]Sce Benedicte with their purses intact.

Fastrada continues. "I believe you intend to advance through
[3]Puntremel en route to the City of Saint Peter."

Feo nods, still trying to recover from the initial jolt caused by
this unsettling yet titillating encounter. "What barriers or difficul-
ties might we face?"

"Dangers to person and purse. The [5]Obertenghi [18]Margrave
has a long and greedy reach. To make it worse, the [15]magistrate
has recruited locals who act as toll collectors, but in fact they are
brigands, demanding much more than the magistrate's toll and
stuffing their own pockets. They take what they want and can be
brutal in their methods."

As Feo is considering what she has said, she continues.
"While it is true that I had no previous knowledge of your
mission other than what I told you was made known to me,
today at the street market I overheard the magistrate's men
saying *pellegrini* (pilgrims) were sighted during their respite at
[1]Sancti Benedicti. They will be looking for you as you approach
Puntremel."

Feo's mind is racing. The retinue is in danger! He must make
haste. Fastrada is aware of his urgent intention as he hurriedly
turns to leave, and she grabs his arm. "Wait! There is a small
[19]chapel beside a [20]stone farmhouse outside Puntremel at [21]San
Cristoforo. Your *pellegrini* will be safe there."

Feo stops his urgent retreat and turns to face Fastrada.

Dare I trust her? It will be late afternoon by the time I collect Sigeric and the others. A wrong decision could lead us into peril, the least of which would be loss of money. No time to waste. The magistrate's men could be headed toward the travelers. The words of her song...no coincidence this!

Reading his mind, Fastrada looks into his eyes and tells him, gently but with conviction. "You will find sanctuary at the [20]farmhouse in [21]San Cristoforo. It is not a place known to the brigands who work for the magistrate. We use it for circumstances like this." At this moment, Feo perceives truth and goodness. She tells him, "Lead them along the path that branches upward off the main trackway and use the little bridge to cross the [22]Gordana. It will twist and turn up a steep hillside. At the top of the hill, there are two large oaks. Hidden between a rock and the base of the tree on the left you will find directions to the [19]chapel with a [20]stone farmhouse."

Three of the magistrate's men are nearing Sigeric's roadside camp as Feo approaches. He holds back, remaining beyond the clearing to observe from inside a small copse of chestnut and oak trees, noting their heavy weaponry including crossbows and shields. Spears are being readied as they get closer to the campsite. The men are laughing as they recount the deaths of the most recent group of *pellegrini* (pilgrims)who resisted being robbed of everything they carried.

It takes no time for Feo to make his decision. He will kill them here and now before they reach Sigeric's camp. He tosses a stone, aiming it so that it lands barely inside the wooded area where he is standing, creating just enough sound to cause the three men to stop. Then he picks up a fallen tree branch, rustling it gently about 15 yards inside the growth of trees. One of three turns and walks toward the woods to investigate. A second tells him, "Don't bother. It is [23]*cinghiali* (wild boars) rooting for grubs." The inquisitive man disregards his comrade and proceeds into the woods. Concealed behind a tree, Feo unsheathes his knife, waiting until the brigand steps around it. In one unfaltering motion, Feo grabs the hair on the back of the man's head, slams his forehead into the tree trunk to silence him, and slits his throat. Then he waits. Becoming impatient after several minutes, the other two brigands begin to call to their comrade. "He must be taking aim at a wild pig," one of them says as he ventures into the woods to retrieve the hunter, adding as he steps over a fallen tree, "We don't have time for this!" Feo grasps his knife firmly as the second bandit enters the copse of trees. The sight of his comrade lying motionless on the ground beneath a tree, throat cut ear to ear, stops him in his tracks before Feo can lay hands on him. As the bandit turns to run, he yells loudly to alert the one who waits in the clearing. Feo takes aim and throws the knife at close range, burying it deep into the retreating man's upper back. Grabbing a crossbow, the remaining thief charges into the woods toward Feo who is now unarmed. In the split second that his crossbow is raised in Feo's direction, the bowman emits a loud grunt and falls to the ground, an arrow through his neck. A formidable man in a monk's robe stands at the far edge of the clearing, lowering a longbow.

Breathing a sigh of relief, Feo walks briskly toward the portly padre who is crossing the clearing. "Shall I thank you or heaven for the archer's skill?" Diggory does not smile at the apostate's quasi-humorous inquiry, struggling to reconcile his peaceful nature and the Lord's teachings with circumstances in which one must kill or be killed. Out of the corner of his eye, behind him in the woods, Feo catches movement on the ground. The thief with the knife in his back is not dead. He's crawling, attempting to get away. "Pardon me, Father, but I must reclaim a valuable weapon," Feo excuses himself as he sprints back into the woods, pulls the knife out of the man's back, and quickly, proficiently cuts his throat, Diggory arriving just in time to witness the grisly scene.

This is indeed one of the dreaded circumstances that Feo and I knew we must be prepared to face. God forgive us.

[24]"And ye shall pursue your enemies, and they shall fall before you by the sword," recites the friar as he places a hand affectionately on Feo's shoulder.

"The blood of a Viking courses through your veins, intrepid Father," smiles a grateful Feo.

Good-natured levity never lying dormant inside him for long, Diggory is unable to suppress a chuckle at Feo's last remark, inwardly beaming with ancestral pride.

"I happened upon the bloody work of these scoundrels beside a nearby stream while fishing." After a knowing nod from Feo, Diggory continues, "Let us make our way back to the archbishop. He will be getting anxious. I will pray for the souls of the departed as we walk. [23]Cinghiali and wolves will feast upon their corpses, leaving only bones and ligaments, just as they did with the small group of [13]viandanti (pedestrian travelers, pilgrims) who were murdered by these brigands. May God have mercy upon their souls."

It is silently understood that the archbishop, and especially Abbot Hew, will not be told of today's unfortunate turn of events. There is already conjecture, especially on Hew's part, about the woman and baby who have mysteriously joined the group of travelers. At this point, Sigeric and Hew probably believe Feo's soul is doomed to perdition. There's no need to provide them with further evidence of his irredeemable nature, not to mention placing into question Diggory's standing as a man of God. The fact that this bloody intervention saved their lives would have little bearing on judgments by the righteous.

As they cross the clearing, Feo stops. "Wait here," he tells Diggory as he returns to the cluster of trees where they left the three dead men. In a few minutes, he reappears carrying their purses, more precisely the stolen purses of dead pilgrims. Diggory makes no sign of disapproval, solemnly reciting verse, "[25]Gather up the leftover fragments, that nothing may be lost." Nodding as he makes the sign of the cross, he adds, "No need to be wasteful, my son."

On the way back to camp, Feo tells Diggory of his encounter with Fastrada in the village of Arzengio on the outskirts of Puntremel. They will need to give the town wide berth, availing themselves of sanctuary offered at a country chapel and farmhouse in the nearby settlement of [21]San Cristoforo.

His head bowed in sadness, Diggory delivers an update to Feo as they proceed back to camp. "Ferand will soon join Our Lord. His strength has been an inspiration. He will not leave San Cristoforo with us."

FOURTEEN

5 – 9 July 990 A.D.
¹San Cristoforo near ²Pontremoli (Puntremel), Italy

The Sanctuary and the Black Rabbit

HAVING GIVEN ²PUNTREMEL WIDE berth to avoid being sighted by the magistrate's men, Feo sees the tops of the two big oaks looming above the upward-winding country road. He treads up the hill in search of the written directions to the sanctuary, leaving the travelers, Ferand on a litter made of branches and leaves, near the narrow trail under the watchful eyes of Diggory. Just as Fastrada told him, under a mossy rock at the base of the tree on the left there is a small piece of rolled parchment, tied with twine.

> *Down the hill on this country road*
> *³Cappella dei Pellegrini waits.*
> *⁴Sanctuary there you will find*
> *While fatigue from your journey abates.*

One last curve to the left
And descend on the road to the right.
Turn right again through a vineyard
With chapel and stone house in sight.

Feo strides back down the steep footpath from the oaks to the winding hillside track where Sigeric and his retinue are waiting. Evening is approaching, and a soothing spring breeze sweeps up the ridge overlooking [1]San Cristoforo, an obscure [5]*refugio* consisting of a tiny country chapel next to a rock farmhouse. As they continue slowly down the steep road, it curves to the right where the chapel and farmhouse come into sight cradled among sheep, fig and olive trees, and vineyards. Diggory gives silent thanks for the kind guidance of the young woman whom Feo has met and for this welcoming, serene sanctuary, especially now. Ferand is not long for this world.

The accommodations are simple but comforting. After prayers in the tiny chapel, Sigeric and Hew walk across the [6]*campo* (field) that lies between the chapel and the farmhouse. Hew has been biding his time, waiting for an opportunity to reinforce any doubts Sigeric might have about Feo's character. "One cannot help but wonder the truth behind the woman Aemilia and the infant. Feo would have us believe he happened upon her on the road near Pavia while we were at the church paying homage to saints. If that was the case, why did she not appear until the next morning?"

Sigeric continues walking, head bowed, as he responds thoughtfully, "Feo said she was fleeing a cruel land baron, that circumstance being the reason he chose to return under darkness to retrieve her. I see no reason to question his account."

"Your Grace, my sincere intention is merely to make you aware of misgivings. Feo's reputation as an apostate gives one pause. It is likely that the woman is not who we have been led to believe she is. Why did Feo not take her to the church for assistance? What will they think in Rome when we arrive with this woman and baby? Their presence among your retinue is bound to raise questions."

Sigeric's face remains expressionless, but his delivery is uncharacteristically brash. "I have known Feo since he was a child, therefore I am aware of his infamy as well as his considerable intellect and talent. I will consider your words and remain vigilant, but he is invaluable to our journey and to the church. Regardless of whether Feo has told the truth, what else would we do with a mother and infant but take them with us? Even if there is an untold story from Pavia, what would we do differently?" Interrupting their stride, Sigeric pauses to glare directly into Hew's eyes. "There is often wisdom and virtue in silence, especially when no good can come of disclosing truth."

Hew feels the sting of the archbishop's displeasure and holds his tongue as they arrive at the quaint stone farmhouse, mulling over other approaches he might use to undermine the loose cohesiveness between the archbishop and his esteemed however infamous aide-de-camp. They are bound by history and immediate purpose, not by righteous mission. Hew smirks as he plots silently.

Left to his own rogue methods, Feo could place Sigeric outside the good graces of the Pope and the powerful malefactors who surround him…actually a fortunate situation that could work to my benefit.

A supper of bread, savory chestnut and chickpea soup, and spit-roasted [7]*cinghiale* is eaten in the farmhouse taverna on the lower floor near the front of the stone structure. Some meat is boiled for broth, and Ferand, in an ever-weakening state, is propped up to sip it.

Diggory and Feo both know that it would be wise to remain here at [1]San Cristoforo for a few days, not only because of Ferand's impending death but also because it is certain that bands of the magistrate's thieves are scouring the roads around [2]Puntremel looking for the [8]pellegrini who eluded them at [9]Cisa Pass—or worse yet that the three dead brigands have been found—another reason it was wise to take their money, creating a picture of murder and theft by other roadway pirates.

While sleeping quarters are being prepared, Feo seeks out Sigeric who is strolling the south vineyard, thankfully without his frequent tail, the spider Hew. "Good evening, Archbishop."

"And to you, Feo. I am enjoying this quiet and peaceful sanctuary."

"Yes, Your Grace, precisely why I would speak with you. Fitting word 'sanctuary,' and let us hope it remains so for our stay here. During the scouting expedition into the village of [10]Arzengio, I learned that the local magistrate's men collect much more than tolls, lining their own pockets and even killing to get what they want. We had the good fortune to slide past the magistrate's troupe at [9]Cisa Pass. They are now looking for us along the routes around [2]Puntremel. It would be advisable to remain at this *refugio* and off the roads for a few days."

"The Lord will watch over us and protect us as we proceed toward the Vatican."

Fatigued by the day's events, Feo responds before he can check his tongue. "This is [11]Lunigiana, Land of the Moon, a legendary and mystical place. We would fare just as well to rely on its magical moon for protection. We must watch out for ourselves and take precautions by remaining out of sight until it is safe to be on the roadways."

At this moment, Sigeric recalls Hew's misgivings about the apostate Feo who immediately regrets his knee-jerk reaction, adding, "I just spoke with Diggory. It appears that the Lord has made the decision for us. Ferand has requested the [12]Viaticum. Surely we will remain here to allow his passing in the comfort of this sanctuary and burial in the [3]Cappella dei Pellegrini cemetery."

A premature demise for the frail and aged Ferand, his death hastened by ill-timed fasting in the name of a loving and merciful God, my dear Archbishop.

✦

As brilliant stars and a large three-quarters moon appear in a blue velvet sky above the Apennines in the [11]Land of the Moon, the weary travelers bed down on straw for their first night in the stable on the lowest level of the hillside farmhouse, their sleeping pallets separated from the animals only by a wooden half-wall. In spite of Feo's fatigue, sleep does not come for what seems like a long time. Diggory is snoring loudly, and Fastrada is on Feo's mind. She is attractive, not stunningly beautiful, but he is bewitched by her. He senses there is much more to this young woman and hopes to see her again during the stay here at [1]San Cristoforo. His thoughts become dream-like as he drifts off to sleep. The remaining bit of powdered [13]mandrake that he added to his wine brings sleep filled with sensual fantasy…. Touching her silken chestnut hair and caressing her breasts, he drifts into a suspended state of erotic reverie.

Looking into her intoxicating green eyes, I caress her flesh and channel her thoughts, a knowing that cannot be…an intimacy that goes beyond this lifetime. Or is it the [13]mandrake root creating vivid sight and touch in a dream? Beware, Feo! Maintain your distrust of emotional intimacy that can dull one's reason.

His resistance fades as she removes her dress.... When he awakens, his only recollection of euphoria is a short, lyrical conversation with Fastrada in the dream that reveals his attraction and his reluctance. [14]"A devil's laugh, a fairy's cry. My emotions are mixed, no wonder why."

As if stepping out of Feo's dream, Fastrada appears in the farmhouse taverna the next morning during breakfast. It takes only one glance between them to communicate, without words, that they need to talk privately. Feo excuses himself to walk in the vineyard near the chapel. Fastrada waits for several minutes before she follows. Walking toward him, she catches her breath as she appraises the tall, slim figure leaning against a cherry tree at the edge of the vineyard. Feo speaks to her in a sincere and gentle voice. "May I express gratitude on behalf of the archbishop and his retinue? This place is the perfect sanctuary for weary [15]*viandanti* (travelers, pilgrims), particularly those who have reason to remain off the road and out of sight for a while."

In a manner that confirms Feo's impression of her, Fastrada responds, "Yes. The path from [2]Puntremel is easily traversed by [15]*viandanti,* yet it's just far enough into the countryside to provide a measure of seclusion. Your decision to remain here for a few extra days is a wise one. A small group of the magistrate's toll collectors has been found robbed and left dead between [9]Cisa Pass and [10]Arzengio." A furtive glance by Fastrada at the sheathed knife hanging from Feo's waist lets him know that she is aware of what actually happened. Without a moment's hesitation, Feo cocks his head to the side, grins mischievously, and says, "Little doubt that discovery has resulted in increased patrolling of the roadways. They are looking for the scoundrels who did this, of course. Ironic, isn't it, that thieves have robbed and killed the thieves who robbed and killed innocent sojourners? [16]Sweet irony. Some would call it justice."

His sarcasm, actually a near confession delivered with a wry half smile, is received by Fastrada with subdued pleasure. Suppressing a grin, she changes the subject, all the while hearing a joyous internal voice telling her that this man—his moral compass, intellect, and humor—have been needed in her life for such a long time.

"I noticed the woman and baby in your entourage. The infant is very young. They seem out of place on a long, hard pilgrimage to the Vatican." Considering the current situation and the distance between Pavia and San Cristoforo, Feo quickly decides it is safe to share that truth as well. This woman Fastrada has an uncanny way of knowing what she couldn't possibly know anyway, not to mention his intuitive trust in her motives and her integrity. "Aemilia gave birth to her daughter Nysa alone, locked in a dank cell at the rear of a church on our route. She was to be sold on the slave market in Venice and the child was to be raised to an age when she would bring a good price."

"I see," acknowledges Fastrada, disgust visible on her face.

"Taking them into Rome would be ill advised" adds Feo. "It would only result in questions and unfounded inferences that would not reflect well on the new archbishop, nor would it bode well for mother or baby. Rome is brimming with amoral, lawless miscreants in high places."

There is no reluctance in Fastrada's offer. "She may remain here if she agrees. We have need of help at the [4]farmhouse. She and the baby will be well cared for, but it would be best if she continues here without 'Sister' before her name, as she has done while among your *pellegrini*, to avoid explanations to the chapel priest—and even better if she can forget she was ever a nun and conceal any connection with her past."

It is no surprise to Feo that the prescient Fastrada knows that Aemilia is a nun even though he did not tell her. "I will speak with her about your generosity and benevolence. She will undoubtedly be grateful for a wholesome environment and safety for herself and Nysa. Pardon my inquisitive nature, but you said 'we.' What is your role at the farm and [3]Cappella dei Pellegrini?"

"The last several years have sensitized me to the deplorable and often hopeless condition of humanity and the shortcomings of the very institution that speaks to the masses of a loving, forgiving Savior. Aemilia and the baby are an egregious example. The church has not been a source of hope or help in my life. There are others around [2]Puntremel, inside the church and in the community, whose observations and experiences have been much like my own and who are willing to do this work. We have quietly committed to helping those whom we can help." Feo's attention to her words is undivided as she continues. "I have dedicated my life to supporting those most in need. I do this by providing assistance here in [1]San Cristoforo at the [3]chapel and [4]farmhouse where *viandanti* (travelers, pilgrims) may avoid being robbed by local authorities and their unscrupulous emissaries in and around Puntremel. I also lend a hand at the [17]lazaretto near Arzengio."

Feo's mind and heart are intently engaged as Fastrada speaks of her life and purpose. "That explains your presence at the Mass of Separation at the grave near [10]Arzengio. I was watching from the woods." Fastrada's response is delayed as her facial expression morphs into a painful affect. "Ah...that is a complicated set of circumstances."

Rather than probe, Feo waits for her to continue. "The man who was declared a leper is my husband, although we have not lived as husband and wife for the past five years. I do not believe he has leprosy, but it makes no difference. The situation suits me, and his condition is without cure regardless."

<hr />

Fastrada waits at dusk midway down the steep ravine leading to the [18]Gordana River behind the farmhouse, gazing at small vineyards on the upward hillside slope above the opposite bank with its cypress and chestnut trees. She has approached the river from the rear of the chapel to avoid being seen.

It is as if my entire life has led me to this moment, to meeting this man Maffeo...Feo...hardly a chance encounter. This is destiny, joyous providence. I can sense that he feels our connection as I do. Intertwined spirits we are, but it feels as though our moments together will be very few.

The sound of small stones and chunks of soil tumbling down the ravine breaks her thoughts as Feo effortlessly descends toward the bracken-covered ledge where Fastrada sits near a rocky drop-off to the river. [19]Stretti di Giaredo, secluded and mystical, not far from here, is the perfect place for lovers. In the moonlight it will provide intoxicating ambiance for their first rendezvous. There are no words, no need for words, during their walk to the canyon under the Lunigiana moon.

As Fastrada unties the strip of leather holding back Feo's long black hair, each can feel the other's heart beating. Lying face to face, their ecstasy begins, spirits forever linked. There are no words as they lie in each other's arms under the stars on a carpet of grass near the water's edge, silver and gold moonbeams dancing on the water's translucent surface, its hypnotic trickling and swooshing through rock outcroppings soothing and lulling the lovers during an embrace that belongs to this magical place and the eons that formed it.

They leave the [19]canyon just before daybreak, timing their walk so that Feo will arrive back at the sanctuary before the travelers are up and about. Their thoughts and emotions, indeed the very air around them, are heavy with shared bliss that is overshadowed by impending separation...perhaps forever. "What shall we do?" Fastrada asks, already knowing the answer. As Feo begins to speak, she interrupts, not wanting him to tell her what she already painfully realizes—that he will proceed to Rome and that the likelihood of his return is improbable. Looking for another topic, but even more so desiring to share with Feo the yet untold story of her circumstances, Fastrada begins, "I told you that my husband, in name only, is doubtfully a leper. I would like to tell you the reason I described him as I did."

Oh, please...no explanation needed or wanted! I care not whether you are married and hope you don't believe I'm a pious prude who would judge you.

Perceiving that Fastrada is earnest, needing to get this explanation off her chest, Feo remains quiet as they walk and she speaks to him of her marriage to a cruel, unfaithful man. Her voice coarsens as she recalls how she became aware of her husband's infidelities, all the while trying to live day-to-day through the unprovoked anger and the beatings he unleashed. Unable to restrain himself, Feo interjects, "Quite frankly, I'm surprised that you were not made aware of his nature by the unknown source that so often makes you aware of what you would not otherwise know." His expression imparts his sincerity, thereby dismissing any inclination Fastrada might have to consider his remark sarcastic or critical.

"Cursed be the silence of that unknown source! It might have saved me much suffering had I known when I met him," she responds. "But the good that has come of it is my strength, resolve, and independence."

"Aye," nods Feo with a kind and gentle expression, placing his arm around her shoulders.

Continuing, she tells him, "I believe his ailment is not leprosy but [20]syphilis, eruption of the flesh being a cardinal sign of both conditions. His ailment was conferred upon by a jury consisting of a priest, a couple of villagers, and a leper. I must admit that I made no attempt to intervene or argue on his behalf when they pronounced him a leper."

"I hope you feel no remorse about that," Feo counsels.

"Any regret I might feel is lessened by the fact that I have voluntarily shared his estate with him. I inherited everything when he went to the [17]lazaretto. I gave him a pouch of money at the gravesite. He was not wealthy but had saved a moderate [21]scrip from the sale of livestock and the produce yielded on rented land."

Following a long embrace, Fastrada takes the path along the ridge above the [18]Gordana leading through neighboring farms and sheep yards into Puntremel. Watching until she disappears on the path's downward descent, Feo strides across the north [6]*campo* (field) of the sanctuary just as day is breaking. The figures of Sigeric, Hew, and Diggory become visible as he nears the farmhouse. This cannot be good. They should not be outside at this early hour. Surprisingly, no one inquires where Feo has been, not that they don't wonder. Feo can't help but think he must look changed, aglow.

"Our dear brother Ferand has joined Our Lord," Diggory announces solemnly as Feo approaches the three.

Sigeric adds, "I shall speak with the priest at Cappella dei Pellegrini about a mass and burial." He walks across the vineyard toward the chapel with the ever-clinging Hew close at his heels.

The next two nights find Feo and Fastrada together at the [19]canyon. Although it is unspoken, they both sense the tragic nature of their relationship, star-crossed lovers cherishing each moment together as if it is their last. In spite of his past ability to maintain a barrier between his innermost thoughts and feelings and his female companions, Feo finds himself more challenged than ever, struggling to keep Fastrada at a safe distance. It is unsettling, however strangely comforting, that this woman probably knows everything about him without being told, including the circumstances surrounding his birth and raising. After all, she knew that he would arrive here as the navigator of a pilgrimage with an archbishop. It is even more unsettling to think that, unlike previous relationships, he might not be in control this time.

I have always limited the nature and duration of my relationships with women, but this woman Fastrada delves into my spirit with a sweet, enchanting power so strong that it is beyond my capacity to limit her reach. Cursed sweet destiny. I feel a joyous, magnetic pull toward her, knowing that all roads have led me to her since the day of my birth.

We are fatefully entangled. I fear that this brief time together is all we will have.

　　　⌒～

On the morning of departure from [1]San Cristoforo, Feo is wandering the sanctuary grounds before dawn, in dread of his parting with Fastrada...even as he admonishes himself for his vulnerability where she is concerned.

In three short nights, she has become my home and my life. She peers unbidden into my flawed soul without judgment. Will fate grant us a future? If one can believe that destiny is known to us on some deep, often imperceptible level, I feel that I belong here with her and yet sense that we will not be given that future, not in this lifetime. Uncertainty! No need to tell her what I am certain she knows... I am on a collision course with realities that encircle me.

The surroundings are clearly visible in milky pre-dawn luminescence as Feo lingers on the north [6]*campo* (field) of the sanctuary with the Apennines looming before him under a huge, dangling half-moon. Then he sees it—the motionless [22]black rabbit sitting upright at the edge of the rocky drop-off to the river. It is unblinking...staring...watching him...but more than that. It seems to beckon, either bidding him onward, over the precipice...or as a harbinger...an omen or perhaps a guide?

I cannot blame this apparition on mandrake root or too much wine last night. Between the ominous black hare and my recurring dreams of a place unknown and yet familiar...towering buildings with broken windows, desperate people, my face painted white, and loud, wailing stringed instruments...I am certain my life is nearing a juncture, a turning point or rebirth that I do not understand...an end but not final? It is eerie and yet not frightening.

"[23]Uht, uht." The silence is broken by a familiar booming voice as a large robed man emerges from the sleeping quarters on the lower level of the house. Feo turns to bid Diggory good morning. When he looks back toward the rocky drop-off to the river, the black rabbit has vanished.

[24]*Strange, it feels as if an eel just slid down my spine.*

Entering the taverna, Feo finds Aemilia and Nysa within, thankfully alone. "Good morning, Aemilia," Feo greets her. "How is the little one?"

"She is doing well, Feo, thanks to you. We are forever grateful. It will be sad indeed to see you leave."

"You are in good hands here. Fastrada will be looking after you both. I have something for you." Feo reaches beneath his tunic and hands Aemilia a pouch. "Hide this under your dress. It must be our secret."

Feeling the coins inside, Aemilia shoots Feo a quizzical glance, touches the pouch to her heart and then quickly hikes up her shift, placing it out of sight as she catches a glimpse of Hew walking toward the taverna entrance. She grimaces and tilts her head in Hew's direction to alert Feo of his approach. Feo winks, leans in toward her, and whispers, "It was donated by some brigands who are no longer able to spend it." He gently places a hand to the baby's cheek, turns and exits, nodding cordially at Hew as they pass at the taverna door.

A squeamish uneasiness grips Fastrada in the pit of her stomach as Feo joins Sigeric's retinue for their departure. Led by Feo, the [15]viandanti (travelers), now three fewer than when they arrived, set out on the lane through the vineyard beside the church and ascend the hill to the road above the farmhouse. Fastrada is shaken, realizing that she is about to experience an emptiness deeper than she has ever known—loss of someone so dear that the rest of her life will feel like a vital part of herself has gone missing. Even though they shared intimate moments, she senses that he withholds much about his life from everyone, including her. He is a man of many talents and strong convictions about justice and humanity, some of which place him at odds with those who surround him.

The coming of this man Feo was felt long before his arrival. I sense his early death. No! **A presence as strong as his cannot just disappear!** *The time and place of our reunion is unknown, however it is certain. Oh, Fate, grant that we will recognize each other when our stars align once again. Providence whispers, giving me comfort that our paths will cross in another time and place. We began an eternity in our numbered hours here.*

Seeking a higher vantage point to capture a last look during Feo's departure, Fastrada runs to the doorway of Cappella dei Pellegrini as the travelers ascend the hill near the small vineyard and approach the winding road that leads back to the Via Romea. As they reach the road at the top, the sound of a [25]psaltery echoing a sad lament from just inside the chapel door drifts up the hillside, its strings weeping, carrying joy and sadness from a lover's heart.

FIFTEEN

Mid–July 990 A.D.
Altopascio near Lucca, Italy

Roadway Rogues

D AYS ON THE ROAD PASS SLOWLY as the *viandanti* (travelers, pilgrims) move steadily southward, most nights
spent in makeshift campsites. At this point, everyone
has heard more than enough of Hew's arrogant and sanctimonious references to [1]Dunstan, former Archbishop of Canterbury,
during the reorganization of Saint Augustine's Abbey. Sigeric
cannot help but ponder the motives and ambitions underlying
Hew's need to boastfully associate himself with the venerated
Dunstan who reformed the Church of England and returned
monastic life to its abbeys.

*Hew is claiming religious kinship that, in reality, was a loose associa-
tion. It was merely happenstance that he was at Saint Augustine's Abbey
for a period of time when Dunstan was there. It is not as if Hew worked
closely with Dunstan as a driving force behind the abbey's reorganization. It
is undoubtedly strategic that, without directly saying so, Hew less than subtly compares me with my predecessor. Dunstan's path and mine within the
church, from Glastonbury to Canterbury, were the same. Dunstan is iconic,*

103

and Hew's name-dropping appears to be a way to embellish his own status and denigrate mine. How could anyone compare with Dunstan's status and accomplishments?

Feo's mind is on Fastrada, especially during the endless nights, longing to return to San Cristoforo and spend the rest of his life with her. Uncharacteristic! His fondest hope is to have time there to continue his writing and his music compositions. Diggory, always straddling two conflicting worlds, looks on the entire situation with trepidation.

It is early afternoon a couple of days before they expect to arrive at the [2]*spedale* at Altopascio. [3]*Cinghiale* (wild boar) foraging signs have been seen in fields along the road. Feo leaves the retinue to go hunting, taking one donkey with him in case it is needed to carry meat. As much as Diggory wants to accompany Feo on the hunting expedition, it is necessary in this region for one of them to remain with the vulnerable travelers who will continue on their way. Feo will catch up with them, hopefully with fresh meat.

The travelers have gone a short distance when four men emerge from a wooded area onto the road in front of them. Placing his hand on the longbow carried by the rear donkey, Diggory quickly decides against attempting to use it. The men, heavily armed with knives and bows, separate to cover each side of the road with one of them running past the travelers to cover them from behind and the largest man facing the travelers. Diggory steps forward. It is apparent that a mundane greeting or contrived request for directions will not dissuade this group of hardened bandits. Their stern, determined expressions are enough to discourage any attempt at a verbal distraction. In spite of this, and having no option other than to attack them which would be foolhardy, Diggory decides to make a futile appeal to their compassion for the sick. "Good day! We are en route to the ²*spedale* at Altopascio." Pointing to the one pilgrim who is atop one of the donkeys, he continues, "Our dear brother is unwell and in need of care." At that, Diggory is hit straight-on in the forehead with a wooden club by the large man at the front. The monk is knocked to the ground, unconscious.

Feo's hunt is successful, and his trip to rejoin Sigeric's retinue is shorter than anticipated. Seeing them sitting at the side of the road at a location not far from where he left them, without pack animals, startles him. As he draws nearer, he sees Diggory reclining against a tree, holding his head in his hands. Stunned expressions turn into looks of relief as the travelers see Feo approaching. His first action is to remove Diggory's hands from his forehead and pour water over the bleeding wound from the skin water vessel he carries. Still quite dazed, Diggory stammers, "Fortunate to have kept our ⁴vestments are we. Even more fortunate to have kept our lives. I attempted a plea for a sick pilgrim. Unwise strategy."

With Feo's return, everyone begins to take stock of what is left—nothing but their robes and shoes—lamenting their dire circumstances with at least two days' travel to the ²*spedale* at Altopascio without supplies. Sigeric prays aloud. Hew, a vile countenance on his chiseled face, offers his own prayer in an unveiled attempt to out-do the archbishop. "Oh Lord, grant us safe passage and protection from our enemies, those who would impede our pilgrimage to the City of Saint Peter in Your name and to Your glory. Grant us the strength to endure the hardships of this journey and the humility to accept our limitations in our quest to become ever more worthy." Feo sees impatience on the faces of the group along with general disregard for Hew's vainglorious behavior.

How's that for arrogant one-upmanship? Hew's continuous attempts at self-aggrandizement are nearly unbearable. What must Sigeric be thinking? His silence and tolerance are admirable, traits that have served him well in the church. They will serve him well in this situation, also. The plotting, ambitious Hew will be undone by his own methods. One can only wonder what obsequious and embarrassing behaviors he will demonstrate in the presence of the Pope...if we even see His Illustrious Holiness during our visit. What is of more concern, however, is to what nefarious lengths Hew might go to gain the favor of the Pope as he lusts for a bishop's mitre...or greater.

As if he hears Feo's thoughts, Diggory, now upright, rolls his eyes with a displeased look that is immediately replaced with a wide smile as he bellows, "Saints be praised and the hunter be blessed! I see a boar pulled behind that donkey! Destitute we may be, but least we shall eat!"

It is apparent there will be no further travel today. The group, Diggory in particular, needs to recover from the attack. While a fire and roasting spit are being prepared, Feo speaks with Sigeric about their situation. "The remaining money that is sewn into the cowls of robes for safekeeping is inadequate to complete the journey. Most of our money was hidden under false bottoms on the [5]confit jars and between the doubled sides on the water skins. All those are gone. Worse yet, the brigands took all the food and pack animals."

"This is a dark and trying hour indeed," agrees the archbishop. "If we can at least make it to the [2]*spedale* at Altopascio, the kindness and generosity of the brothers there, who are dedicated to the aid of *pellegrini* (pilgrims), will provide us with the resources to continue on to Rome."

"It would be comforting indeed, Your Grace, if we could depend on the largesse of the friars at the [2]*spedale*, however we cannot. [6]The political and financial circumstances of the brothers at Altopascio are unstable since the transfer of power in favor of the Franks. [7]Given the ongoing rivalry and antagonism between the papacy and the Holy Roman Emperor, the [2]*spedale's* allegiance to the church and its adherents cannot be taken for granted."

A sullen look washes over Sigeric as he grasps the reality in Feo's counsel and responds, "So be it. We shall proceed to Altopascio with guarded expectations. God help us." Feo, however, considers the alternatives.

God help us? We must help ourselves. We cannot continue forward or turn back toward England in our current circumstances.

Before dusk as the travelers are using whatever they can find to cook the pig and assemble makeshift sleeping pallets using foliage, Feo leaves the campsite without explanation, taking just the bow and knife he had taken hunting and a length of rope. He is hoping to catch enough daylight to find his way across fields and through wooded areas in the direction the thieves must have taken. A worried Diggory watches, thinking he should go with Feo who has made his way across the roadway and is sprinting through a field of ankle-high clover dotted with clusters of narcissus. The others look on also, choosing not to question or discourage Feo's departure. He is deep in thought as he approaches the woods.

The men who robbed us are predators, prowling the roadways and pouncing on pilgrims who carry money, supplies, and valuable relics. My guess is that they keep close to their quarry, using one or two campsites not far off this road to watch for travelers.

Feo plans carefully as he proceeds deep into a wooded area looking for signs of human and donkey movement through the bracken, twigs, and leaves. Finding what he believes could be their trail, he considers how he might reclaim the money, donkeys, and other goods as he walks softly and quickly. Diggory said there are four of them, heavily armed. Feo weighs the probability of the outcome.

If ever I could use the help of a Viking warrior, it is now. However, that cannot be. The entire group of travelers must be aware of my intentions and what must take place in order to regain what was taken by the thieves. If and when I return with pack animals, money, and supplies, there will be no doubt of what has taken place. With Hew's presence, Diggory's life in the church would be jeopardized if he has any involvement in what I'm about to do.

It is heavy dusk when Feo smells a campfire and hears voices beyond the forest edge. He stops, keeping out of sight yet near enough to observe. Their camp is just beyond the trees, set up in a semi-circle with sleeping pallets facing a fire pit. The donkeys are tethered at the edge of the woods just to the north but hopefully far enough away to prevent braying at the arrival of a visitor during the night.

Feo leans back against the base of a large oak and waits until the four thieves are asleep. As he tiptoes closer, still within cover and taking care not to step on twigs and fallen branches, he hears at least two of the men snoring. He decides to start with the other two, hoping their struggling can be silenced and that if the snorers are awakened, that they will be dazed, their response time delayed. A full moon lights up the clearing around the campsite. Approaching stealthily, Feo notes that one of the men, the largest one, is lying on his side facing the woods. This one might be apt to think any noise coming from the man on the other side of the fire—if Feo can stifle the noise to grunting—is just the sound of a sleeping comrade. So Feo makes his way to the snoring man who is lying on his back on the opposite side of the campfire which is now merely glowing embers. In one fluid move, Feo covers the thief's nose and mouth with one hand as he cuts his throat with the other. Holding his grip on the nose and mouth firmly with both hands to muffle the gurgling, Feo crouches, barely breathing beside the dying man, watching the pulsating fluid run onto the dirt and the color drain from his face under the moonlight. After a few minutes have passed and the crimson stream is just a slow ooze without any movement by the thief, Feo begins to crawl silently toward his next snoring victim-to-be. He pulls back suddenly when the man rolls onto his back, mumbling something unintelligible. Heart pounding, thinking he could soon be overtaken by three thieves, Feo stops and waits.... To his amazement, the man continues to sleep and mumble, dreaming. Closing his eyes as if to give thanks for another back-lying sleeper, Feo repeats what he did to the first one.

Two dead, two to go. Will my luck hold or will this venture end my journey? Odds are not in my favor.

Just before Feo gets within reach of him, the third thief snorts loudly, waking himself with his own snoring, and sits up. Seeing the dark intruder near him, he springs to his feet. Feo leaps onto the man, attempting to silence him, but it is too late. "Help! Ermo! Wake up!" As Feo and the man struggle, the fourth thief, the largest one who is lying facing the woods, is awakened. Sleep groggy, the big man stands unsteadily in a half-sleep state, continuing to face the woods where a crashing sound is heard in the dark just beyond the edge of the trees, diverting his attention to the direction of the forest and distracting him from the voice that woke him and the fight taking place near the fire pit. At that very moment, a rope is thrown around his neck from the back and tightened by a pair of large, meaty hands. As his moonlit countenance turns blue, the sound of his wheezing is broken by a familiar, deep voice. "Heaven forgive me, but you, big fellow, nearly killed me and my head still throbs." After a short time, the thief's gasping and wheezing cease, he drops to the ground, and the same large hands remove the rope from his neck.

Turning his attention to the ongoing hand-to-hand combat on the opposite side of the fire pit, Diggory notices that Feo's knife has been dropped out of his reach. Stepping behind the remaining crook who is now atop Feo, the friar slips the rope around his neck and tightens it. The headlock grip on Feo is released, and within minutes the last thief lies among the other three on the ground around the fire pit.

As he re-ties the rope belt around his ample waist, Diggory hears Feo say, "Such brilliant trickery, Father, to throw that rock from the fire pit over the head of the big man and into the woods beyond! You saved us both from being pummeled by that behemoth. Did I hear you say he is the one who knocked you unconscious?" Diggory does not respond with words. He throws his big arms around Feo, lifting him off his feet and hugging him as a father would embrace a child who has survived some crisis.

As they gather all the goods that were stolen and use the long rope Feo brought to tether the donkeys together, Diggory says, "I waited until after dark, and hopefully the pilgrims were asleep, before following you. The full moon is a blessing this night. Let us not forget to also reclaim the weapons they stole from us." He winks and adds, "A Viking prefers his longbow, not the rope belt of a monk."

With a loving, grateful expression, Feo responds, "I have never been so relieved as when you appeared. Without you, I would be dead and Sigeric would not make it to Rome or back to England. On the other hand, you could pay a dear price for saving me and the archbishop's pilgrimage. Make haste back to camp, hopefully to lie as if asleep near the campfire before day-break. Later, the retinue will know that the brigands did not hand over their spoils willingly, but they will not protest the return of the supplies and money that will enable us to continue on to Rome. They already suspected what I was going to do, and of course no one questioned where I was going or tried to stop me. Even if the archbishop feigns ignorance of the bloodshed that has taken place, the robed spider Hew will surely relate this incident as an example of the wayward and sinful ways of an apostate who is trusted by a naïve archbishop."

Beady, steel-blue eyes are watching as Diggory arrives back at the campsite shortly before dawn and lies down as if sleeping near the cold campfire.

The sun has been up for over an hour when Feo arrives with donkeys in tow, packed with all the supplies that were stolen including the money concealed under false bottoms on [5]confit jars and in double-sided water skins. The travelers express their gladness and relief that they will be able to continue the jour-ney. No questions are asked, silent acknowledgement that every-one knows what Feo must have done to reclaim the goods, even though he stopped at a stream to wash the blood from his knife, hands, and arms. The only tell-tale signs of violence are a bruise near Feo's eye and his badly swollen right hand. After a breakfast of tea and porridge, the group sets back on the road toward the [2]spedale at Altopascio in the proximity of Lucca.

As they have done more and more frequently since leav-ing Canterbury, Feo's thoughts turn to the ironies in life and his belief that this expedition does not align with his higher aspirations. The dangers, most of which seem incomprehensible to Old Sobersides—or more likely he is intentionally blind and deaf—will continue, and so will the web that is being spun by Hew.

Destiny and my desired pursuits are competing forces. I was born into circumstances that have provided me with rare opportunities to hone the skills of a statesman and an artist even as I am bound to this false purpose. Irony! And the recurring, fleeting images…so real…sights and sounds in a faraway place, but more than that…the feelings attached to them…familiar and yet to come? Ongoing struggles beyond this time and place? Fate. This will not end well.

SIXTEEN

26 July 990 A.D.
¹Sce Flaviane, Italy

The Spider's First Bite

SIGERIC'S RETINUE IS NEARING ROME. Feo estimates their arrival to be in six days. The stay at Altopascio was cordial and uneventful, Sigeric quietly noting that conditions at the *spedale* (hostel, hospital) would lead him to agree with Feo's assessment of prevailing loyalties. The environment was supportive of *pelligrini* (pilgrims) as long as their needs were limited to meals and respite from travel. The travelers having recovered all their money and supplies, nothing more was needed or requested.

The travelers stop late in the afternoon to set up camp for the night. Sigeric takes a leisurely stroll in a nearby field with several of the others, including Hew of course, who is never far from the archbishop. It isn't long before Hew comes trotting back to camp, dancing as he lifts his robe, stopping every few steps to bend down and rub his ankles. "On fire! My ankles are burning!" It isn't long before two others return, grimacing and pointing to their lower legs. Looking at Hew's ankles, Diggory tells all of them, "Don't scratch or rub. You have walked through [2]stinging nettle in the field." With that, the monk walks briskly toward the field where he bends over and appears to be picking something. After several minutes, he returns with both hands full of dandelions and distributes them among the agitated, stung walkers. "Rub the milky liquid from inside the stems on your legs and ankles to relieve the burning." Within minutes, the nettle victims are no longer kicking their legs in distress. Sigeric smiles uncharacteristically as he observes.

Evenings on the road can be long, particularly in the company of an irritating sycophant. This evening, rather than read from his prayer book, Hew is preoccupied with their proximity to the Vatican. He is anticipating the interactions that will take place with [3]John XV and the dignitaries who surround him. As usual, Sigeric remains quiet, allowing Hew to conjecture, all the while unintentionally painting a picture of his own obsequious character, his underlying motives exposed through erudite statements that reveal a dangerously ambitious man. His chatter is incessant and is exhausting everyone's patience. "Your ordainment, Archbishop, is indeed an honor for all of England. The [3]Holy Father will undoubtedly have made arrangements for our arrival. The ceremony will surely be attended by all his cardinals."

Sigeric's response is terse and stern, his tone clearly intended to curtail Hew's prattle. "Whatever the event will be, the fulfilled journey will be to the glory of God."

One glance between Diggory and Feo communicates their mutual thoughts. Contrary to his even-tempered disposition, Diggory has reached the limit of his tolerance. To make matters worse, darkness has fallen, so there is no escape from the present company.

Hew is insufferable! Methinks the abbot's ambition is outmatched only by his stupidity. Does he have any awareness of the transparency of his behaviors? His insatiable need for recognition and advancement is rapidly surpassing his judgment. As we get closer to the City of Saint Peter, his behavior will only become more unbearable.

Choosing not to recognize Sigeric's less than subtle enough-is-enough assertion, Hew brazenly continues, "The Holy Roman Catholic Church will provide us with the acknowledgement and confirmation that we deserve." At this, Diggory's teeth are set on edge.

"Us"? "We"? There is obviously some confusion about the purpose of the consecration and who will receive the pallium.

No longer able to restrain himself, Diggory targets Hew with an intense, piercing glare as he speaks in a deliberate tone through clenched teeth, "We? The archbishop alone will receive the pallium. As for acknowledgement and confirmation, those petty concerns not only diminish the intended purpose of the consecration, but also the glory of God."

Hew's toxic smirk, followed by the first silence from him since sundown, confirm what Diggory and Feo already know—that Diggory has now placed himself in the same position Feo has occupied since before they departed Canterbury—outside the graces of this man of the church, a creature who is without grace himself.

As he often does, Feo lies awake after everyone is bedded down for the night. His thoughts are of Fastrada in his arms under the moonlight at [4]Stretti di Giaredo. He hopes for a future together, realizing how unusual these thoughts are for him, the happily footloose loner.

Careful, Feo! There are reasons why you have never committed to any woman. A life without emotional and domestic attachments has allowed time for your greatest passions, music and writing.

He is longing to get back to an untitled story that he left at Glastonbury, a [5]lengthy epic poem written purely for enjoyment about demons, a dragon, and a warrior who becomes a king. He misses composing music and ponders new possibilities...perhaps a piece for Fastrada, a nocturne...humming quietly under his breath as his imagination then turns to writing a story with her as the heroine...or perhaps the femme fatale...when an alarming sound jerks him back to reality.

Sigeric is struggling to speak, voice broken by what sounds like spasms in his throat, his words unintelligible. Rushing to his side, Feo sees Sigeric's panic-stricken eyes in the faint light from the remaining embers of the campfire, drool running down his chin. He is unable to even grasp Feo's hand. A tell-tale clue is barely visible on the ground—a familiar leaf. As Feo props Sigeric's torso to make it easier for him to breathe, Diggory scoops up the dried leaf as he kneels to lend a hand. "[6]Hemlock," the monk mutters under his breath, heard only by Feo and perhaps Sigeric. The startled others gather around the archbishop. Feo directs one of them to bring drinking water, lots of it. "Make haste!" Diggory prays, "Lord, grant him the strength to dilute and weaken that which is stealing his breath." Two of the travelers hold Sigeric upright so that he can drink. Feo pours water into a cup, placing it to Sigeric's lips. "Sip and try to swallow," he instructs Sigeric who is helpless at this point, unable to acknowledge whether he understands as Feo repeatedly tips the cup to allow small amounts of the liquid into the archbishop's mouth. "Good, good," Diggory urges him as he somehow manages to swallow. "You must drink enough water to dilute what contaminates. Sip until you are able to swallow larger amounts!" Hew stands back, feigning shock and concern.

Over the next several hours, the entire retinue remains at Sigeric's side, praying and assisting him to drink as much water as he possibly can. As dawn breaks, it is becoming apparent that tragedy has been averted. Sigeric is drinking water on his own, sitting up and able to speak. Hew, avoiding eye contact with Feo and Diggory, offers a prayer of thanks that Sigeric has been spared and will live to complete his journey to the Vatican to be bestowed with the pallium of the Archbishop of Canterbury.

One of the travelers speculates that Sigeric might have been feeling unwell during supper because he ate very little. This comment offers Hew the perfect opportunity to sidetrack any notion of poisoning. "Oh yes, I noticed his meager appetite, also. Perhaps we ingested some rancid meat. I also felt ill after supper. It might be wise to dispose of the preserved meats."

Dawn is breaking. Feo gives Diggory a sideways nod, indicating that he should follow, and walks out of camp. Waiting for a bit of time to pass so Hew's suspicion will not be aroused, Diggory leaves the campsite in the direction taken by Feo. Across a large field, just beyond the edge of a grove, Feo exclaims, "The taste of hemlock is unpleasant. No wonder Sigeric ate so little for supper."

"Aye, my son, and a blessing it is that the bitter taste hindered his appetite. This is indeed a heinous situation." Diggory reaches into a pocket and pulls out the evidence, a dried [6]hemlock leaf. "Sloppy attempt at murder. It must have been dropped as leaves were hurriedly crushed into Sigeric's food. Are you thinking what

I am thinking about Hew's probable involvement? He would like nothing better than to be rid of Sigeric before we reach the City of Saint Peter."

"Not only am I thinking it," Feo states adamantly, "but I know precisely when and where he obtained the [6]hemlock. We were at the Great St. Bernard Pass. Do you recall a couple of the pilgrims picking what they believed to be cow parsley, but you recognized it as hemlock? Hew returned to the meadow alone that evening. I thought it suspicious at the time."

"Of course!" cries Diggory, holding the palm of his hand to his forehead. "Not only has Hew been pursuing the vacant seat of the Bishop of Ramsbury since Sigeric was appointed Archbishop of Canterbury, but he is ambitious and egotistical enough to believe that he might slither into any upper church vacancy in England including a vacant archbishop's position. In the event of Sigeric's demise, the upcoming audience with the pope would provide Hew with the opportunity to present himself as the available candidate, ever invoking the name of Dunstan as if they were close colleagues. The naked truth is that the self-absorbed [3]John XV cares not a whit about the renowned Dunstan or anyone else. Nor does he care whether Sigeric, Hew, or one of our donkeys receives the archbishop's pallium."

"Yes," Feo adds, "and the Unholy See would readily consecrate a braying ass such as Hew who would eagerly expand John XV's greedy reach into England."

"And all this would take place after papal condolences are given for the death of Sigeric, of course," postulates Diggory.

Cocking his head to the side and giving Diggory a knowing nod, Feo jests, "I knew the moment I met you that you were not merely a handsome Viking." In spite of the gravity of the situation, the monk laughs heartily as Feo continues, "John knows that [7] Æthelred the Unready is a weak and foolish leader, one who is easily misadvised because of his youth and inexperience. Where rulers are weak, monasteries align themselves with the papacy. The current circumstances in England provide an opportunity for [3]John XV and potentially for Hew. The question is how to proceed. I am not sure if Sigeric heard you when you recognized the hemlock. Do you think he would openly declare that Hew tried to kill him?"

"He would not. If he did, we would have no choice but to enter Rome with a criminal in tow. It would cast a dark cloud over Sigeric's reception, not to mention placing his judgment in question. Would an enlightened man not make a better choice about someone who would accompany him? On the other hand, Vatican residents are so accustomed to [8]corruption and deviants that this murder attempt might not negatively impact their opinion of a weak archbishop...or the unscrupulous Hew for that matter. The problem, however, is that Sigeric himself is naïve and idealistic enough to believe it would make a difference in how he is perceived." Diggory's expression is forlorn as he awaits Feo's response.

"So be it. We proceed to Rome under the pretense that the archbishop was made deathly ill by rancid meat. And, dear Father, you and I both know that Hew does not wish either of us well. He is threatened by our discernment."

Feo's thoughts then turn to the archbishop.

Integrity and morality are sacrificed when, through their silence, men of the church show tacit approval of wrongdoing. Sigeric appears naïve, but surely, he must understand the contradictions between appearances and realities. He takes the path of least resistance, the safest and most favorable to his own ambitions. The friction between him and Hew, whose ambitions might even exceed a bishop's [9]mitre, is escalating, much to the disgust and entertainment of all who observe it. I doubt that Hew's behaviors will be tolerated at the Vatican.

As he prepares the for another day on the road, uncertainty and fear of what may lie ahead bear down upon the earthy monk who has found a son in Feo, the formidable and gifted young man who kindles an affection as deep as the pride he instills in those who know him.

SEVENTEEN

9 August 990 A.D.
[1]Ponte Molle north of Rome, Italy

Spins the Spider

THE GABLED SILHOUETTE OF [2]Saint Peter's Basilica and the imposing outline of [3]Castel Sant'Angelo are visible on the skyline to the south as the travelers rest briefly at [1]Ponte Molle, allowing the pack animals to drink in the [4]Tevere (Tiber River).

"Your Grace, we will reach the Vatican by early afternoon, giving us ample time to make our presence known before the evening meal. I would be honored to go before the retinue as your delegate to announce your arrival to church officials." The Abbot Hew nearly bows before Sigeric as if he is an aide-de-camp who wishes to serve His Grace, but he is actually appealing for the opportunity to make a grand entrance as the esteemed emissary of the Archbishop of Canterbury.

"We shall enter Rome together," Sigeric responds resolutely. "Humble servants of God do not require a pretentious announcement." Scanning at the faces of the group, Feo can read their shared thoughts.

At last! Sigeric has finally spoken what he is thinking and shown Hew a boundary line.

"I merely intended to give His Holiness the courtesy of notification of the arrival of honorable guests who have traveled far and to expedite accommodations for your comfort, Archbishop. Would you not anticipate lodging within the [5]*Patriarchium*?"

Sigeric looks to Feo, hoping for an answer to Hew's question. When there is no immediate comment from Feo, Sigeric responds, "Whatever lodging is provided will be gratefully accepted and appreciated."

To reinforce Sigeric's acceptance of whatever accommodations are allocated as well as to set realistic expectations, Feo adds, "Any presumption on our part would be ill advised." His temptation to give further voice to what is known of the low value placed on any church appointee by the Holy See—except to the degree he is useful in the hands of the ecumenical patriarch—is curbed by Hew's presence. There is no need to diminish the importance of Sigeric's ordination or to provide the spider with more venom.

EIGHTEEN

9 August 990 A.D.
The Vatican

Humiliating Reception

THE SUN IS HIGH AND THE AIR is heavy with midday heat when the retinue reaches the Vatican led by Sigeric dressed in a plain undyed robe, walking beside a donkey and carrying a [1]crosier. Stopping near the [2]obelisk, he motions for Feo to come to him, handing over the rope to the donkey.

"Your Grace?"

"I will go alone into the basilica to pray before making our arrival known to the first clergyman I see. Please try to make everyone as comfortable as possible in this unforgiving heat until I return." Glancing in the direction of Hew, Sigeric adds, "And no one is to follow me. I will return with details for our stay." Feo nods and returns to the group as the archbishop proceeds toward St. Peter's Basilica. Hew can hardly restrain himself, nervous excitement surging, evident in his hyper-alert state. He appears ready to pounce on Feo for information, but Feo preempts the inquiry. "Sigeric has asked that we wait until he returns. Shade from the sun is what we need now."

The area surrounding the Vatican does not reflect what would be expected at the door of the Holy Roman Catholic Church. Thoroughfares are crowded and filthy from the constant presence of pilgrims and itinerant merchants who camp here. A place to wait out of the sweltering heat will not be easy to find. Diggory points to a narrow passage between two buildings and directs the travelers, "Over there. Follow me." Leading donkeys behind them, the group steps into the shade of the alley, but they dare not sit because of the rotting garbage and human waste. So, they stand in the shade just inside the entrance of the narrow alley between buildings, resolved to tolerate the sickening odors at least for a while. Attempting to make the best of an unpleasant situation, the amiable Diggory notes, "We have traveled far and overcome some daunting hardships. At least we are out of the blistering sun, in the shadow of St. Peter's Basilica, and our water skins are filled with fresh water from the Tevere."

Unable to remain silent any longer, Hew chides, "We could have been in temperate rooms at the [3]*Patriarchium* if I had come in advance to announce our arrival."

Looking squarely into Hew's eyes, Feo responds with composure, "Where would you have presented yourself to announce the archbishop's arrival? One does not just knock on the door of the *Patriarchium* expecting to be received, and church officials do not linger at the Vatican to pray, much less to receive visitors. Archbishop Sigeric stands a better chance than any of us of receiving a welcome."

Silence from Hew who is steaming—and not from the summer heat—as the travelers suppress chuckles and quench their thirsts from water skins. Hew considers the situation and what he can further expect from the infamous Feo.

Feo lives up to his reputation as a man with a solid grasp on reality and reason. He astutely reads situations and the motives of those who have created them, responding with a cool head and measured words. He is not someone to be trifled with or fooled. I must change my strategy and proceed in a different manner—in the shadows. If [4]John XV also is true to his reputation, he will find my pledge of support from the distant territories of England appealing…in exchange for my eventual appointment as the head of the Church of England.

Their wait, approximately two hours, seems longer than it actually is with Diggory taking periodic walks around the obelisk to watch for Sigeric. When he is spotted crossing the Vatican grounds toward them, he is not alone. He is accompanied by a tall man in a gray robe of fine linen adorned with the black embroidered insignia of the [5]monastic military knighthood. Diggory waves to Feo who leads the anxious retinue out of the alley to reunite with the archbishop. Hew ambles slowly at the rear, his modus operandi having shifted from the role of outward aggressor to subversive mercenary. His behavior change does not go unnoticed by Feo or Diggory.

Evening finds Sigeric and company on the south side of Rome in dormitory-like rooms behind the [3]*Patriarchium* stables. The rooms, intended for guards, are more than adequate and quite comfortable compared to the *refugios* (hostels, shelters) along the Via Romea, although Feo would always prefer to sleep under the stars. Given earlier interactions about accommodations, the *pellegrini* (pilgrims) cannot help but wonder what the suddenly and mysteriously subdued Hew must be thinking about the Archbishop of Canterbury being housed in guards' quarters behind the stables. Diggory is having the same thoughts about the state of the vile abbot's mind as well as the dubious reception so far—possibly a sign of what is to come.

If the sycophant Hew had gone ahead of Sigeric to trumpet our arrival, the lot of us might be camped amidst the filth with the merchants and pilgrims around the Vatican.

After they share a supper with guard staff, Sigeric informs the group of what he understands to be the overall plan. "Tomorrow, our first full day in Rome, we will pray at the Shrine of the Apostle Peter followed by a visit to the English College of Saint Mary. Beyond that, the only other event will be the bestowal of the pallium. That date is undetermined. You should avail yourselves of any desired opportunities for prayer and devotion while here in the City of Saint Peter as soon as possible. Feo, it is my hope that we can begin the homeward journey soon after the ceremony, the following day if possible. I look to you to ready provisions for our departure. Unless other meetings and visits are scheduled, we could begin the return journey to Canterbury sooner than anticipated, making up for the extra days we spent at the sanctuary in San Cristoforo and giving us extra days to clear the mountainous regions to the north well before winter conditions set in."

Sigeric's expression, as always, is flat, however his words and tone belie his disappointment with the lukewarm welcome he has received thus far through trickle-down in the Vatican hierarchy. It takes only a brief look at Hew to see that he is forcibly suppressing the urge to jump and scream, the source of his agitation being unanswered questions about any possible interface with [4]John XV and the cardinals. Fortunately for him, as he struggles to remain silent, one of the others asks, "Is there any indication that we, or at least you, Archbishop, will receive an audience with the pope other than at the ceremony where you will receive the pallium? We have traveled such a great distance. Did you perhaps speak with the His Holiness today?" Sigeric replies, "I did not. Following my prayers in the basilica, my initial encounter was with a priest who happened to be walking through the atrium. He kindly summoned a Vatican guard who, after receiving instructions from church leadership, informed me of the plan that I have now shared with you and then escorted us here to these quarters. We must be patient and allow the Holy See to provide us with a schedule befitting the purpose of our visit."

Sigeric's response, not having eased anyone's anxiety about potentially unrealized expectations, is received with silence on all fronts. Grounded in reality and having no misconceptions about the priorities and focus of church leaders, Feo anticipates the disappointment that he has always known the group might experience.

Prayers at the Shrine of the Apostle Peter and a visit to the English College of Saint Mary—diversions to fill up the English visitors' time. I would not be surprised if the pope delegates bestowal of Sigeric's pallium to a subordinate, perhaps a cardinal. [4]*John XV's precious time is allocated to those who are apt to promote his pecuniary interests. Old Sobersides does not fit that description.*

The retinue has been in bed for a couple of hours, but Diggory cannot sleep. His sixth sense has kicked in. Hearing the door of the sleeping quarters open ever so gently, he sits up just in time to catch the glimpse of a shadowy figure slipping out, leaving the door slightly ajar to prevent making any sound. Sprinting across the dark room to the door, Diggory cracks it just enough to peek out. Hew's profile is clearly visible against the candlelight inside when a guard opens the door to a room on the other side of the narrow corridor.

NINETEEN

10 August 990 A.D.
Rome, Italy

Dubious Ceremony

BEFORE LEAVING FOR THE day's activities, Diggory finds
Feo appraising the fitness of the donkeys. He will not
accompany Sigeric and the retinue to the Shrine of the
Apostle Peter and the English College of Saint Mary, pleased
to stay behind and begin preparations for an anticipated early
departure for England. "You look ill at ease. Did you not sleep
well, Father?"

"I did not!" Diggory snaps angrily. "Wickedness was stirring.
The spider was spinning his web last night." Feo continues his
close examination of the donkeys, not appearing in the least surprised by the news as Diggory continues, "I had miscalculated
the abbot's machinations, expecting him to use incidents involving thee and me to blackmail Sigeric here in Rome or to cast
doubt on Sigeric's prudence and judgment as the Archbishop of
Canterbury, but I had sorely underestimated his insight. Hew has
apparently come to the realization that the Holy See cares not
a wink about any sacrilegious acts we have carried out or about

your reputation as an apostate, so using those against Sigeric will not work. He seems to know that its sole interest is expanding its reach into the pockets of the churches, abbeys, and the struggling masses across Christendom. Hew is in his moral element here. Last night he sneaked out and visited one of the guards after we were all asleep...or so he thought."

"No doubt a guard who will be his liaison with church leaders," Feo adds. "It is fortunate that you witnessed this. We must be more vigilant than ever. I fear for Sigeric's life. Unlike the inept Hew, the mercenary forces here in Rome will not carry out a failed assassination attempt."

⌒

The papal aide who accompanies the retinue to today's scheduled visits informs Sigeric that the ceremony for bestowal of the pallium will take place on 13 August at a side altar in Saint Peter's Basilica. He does not say who will officiate. Sigeric hopes it will be the pope, of course, however he is beginning to wonder if his visit is being ignored by John XV or if the Holy Father is even present in Rome. Pride and humility battling inside him, plus fear of disappointment and embarrassment, do not incline the archbishop to inquire about any details.

TWENTY

13 August 990 A.D.
Rome, Italy and the Vatican

Feo's Fate

THE DAY OF THE BESTOWAL OF THE archbishop's pallium has arrived. In spite of hopes to the contrary, there has been no contact over the past few days, no formal invitation for the Archbishop of Canterbury to be received by the pope or any of the Vatican officials. In the meantime, members of Sigeric's retinue have made their way back and forth between their quarters in the south of Rome, the Vatican, and other revered sites—minus Hew whose absence is conspicuous. Sigeric has continued his well-established routine of evening prayers, a cherished time when he is alone with the Lord. Since the ceremony will take place late this afternoon, almost as an afterthought by the Vatican leaders, he plans to adhere to his routine of prayers at Saint Peter's this evening rather than at the Patriarchium.

Hew has made himself scarce. Sigeric suspects what might be taking place, but in characteristic fashion he has chosen to withdraw in prayer and trust that the Lord will lead him through any impending crisis. If not the Lord, Feo and Diggory will.

The past couple of days have given the navigator and the monk time to plan for whatever might come of the abbot's plot, Hew undoubtedly having aligned himself with the unholy underbelly of the papacy. Sigeric's departure from Rome is planned for tomorrow, and the one predictable time when he can be found alone is during his evening prayers. If an attempt is made on the archbishop's life, it will be tonight.

Sigeric and his retinue try not to show their disappointment when a lone cardinal officiates at the bestowal of the [1]pallium at a side altar. It is a lackluster ceremony intended to diminish the status of the Archbishop of Canterbury, titular head of the Church of England. Following the short ritual during which Hew can hardly subdue a smirk, the group makes its way back to their sleeping quarters on the south side of the city to pass their last night in Rome. Feo and Diggory remain at the Vatican for the alleged purpose of accompanying Sigeric after his evening prayers.

As the prayer hour nears, Diggory pulls Sigeric into a small, curtained niche off the [2]basilica [3]nave. "Forgive me, Your Grace, but you must remove your robe." Without waiting for a response and disregarding Sigeric's look of bewilderment, Diggory lifts the archbishop's robe over his head and hands him trousers, a belt, and a linen shirt. "Put these on. Quickly! Your life is in danger!"

"But...but...my prayers." The resolute look on Diggory's face makes it clear to the archbishop that he must do as he is told, no discussion.

"We must hurry! You will walk out of here a nondescript man of the laity. Feo needs your robe. In lieu of your evening prayers, you might pray for him as we walk." Leaving Sigeric's robe on the floor of the small room for Feo, Diggory stuffs the coveted pallium under his own large robe and leads the stunned archbishop into the nearest of [2]five long aisles and swiftly out of the basilica.

Watching from across the nave as he waits for Diggory to lead Sigeric outside, Feo sees it—the [4]black rabbit—here inside the basilica at the far side of the huge room, staring at him with the same unblinking eyes that beckoned to him from the edge of the steep, rocky decline to the river behind the sanctuary in San Cristoforo. He glances at Diggory and Sigeric who are exiting the far end of the basilica, and when he looks back in the direction of the apparition, it is gone. Somewhat shaken but maintaining his composure and focusing on his immediate purpose, Feo walks briskly across the nave to the curtained niche and slips Sigeric's cowled robe over his clothing.

Three seasoned [5]assassins wait until the archbishop, kneeling silently before the altar with cowl pulled up over his head, is in deep prayer before they close in at his back. Sensing their approach, Feo recalls a time in his early twenties when he endured many months of grueling hand-to-hand combat training with an English warrior, one who defended the territories during Viking raids. He hopes those skills will serve him as well now as they did during the journey to Rome…even though he is quite certain the black rabbit is the harbinger of his death.

Astonishment washes over on the faces of the three killers as Feo turns to face them, cowl no longer concealing his face, and they realize that the man before them is not the meek and vulnerable Sigeric. They carry not knives but combat weaponry, Roman [6]*gladii* (swords).

⌒

Diggory shepherds the archbishop past the Vatican [7]obelisk and into the morass of camps that surround it. Intending to return to the sleeping quarters in the south of Rome, Sigeric must again yield to the stern insistence of the monk. "No, Your Grace. You would not be safe at the *Patriarchium*. Those who would harm you will look for you there. The Vatican soldiers are there. In truth, you are not safe anywhere in Rome. Tonight, for your own wellbeing, you must remain a nondescript person among the pilgrims and merchants who camp here." Finding a patch of downtrodden grass among the campsites, Diggory hurriedly instructs Sigeric, "Remain here until I come back for you. I pray that the others—and Feo—will accompany me on my return. Have faith and patience. It could take hours."

An ordinary man sits alone amidst the campsites as darkness falls. Diggory barrels back toward Saint Peter's where several perplexed pilgrims are standing at the doors, wondering why the entrance is locked, apparently bolted from the inside. Pouring sweat, his chest heaving from exertion, Diggory puts all his considerable weight behind several futile attempts to force open the massive doors. In despair and fearing the worst, he collapses against the doors as his body to slides downward until he is slumped on the portico floor, face in hands.

My son, my son…. God be with you! I have never felt so helpless against mine enemies!

⌒

The three veteran [5]assassins are awestruck at Feo's skill in fending them off with a weapon that is only a fraction the size of theirs. He swerves and dodges and leaps over their swords, each time piercing them in vital spots—throat, upper chest—as they lunge at him. His youth and agility prove too much for two of them. The third assassin seizes this opportunity to maneuver behind Feo. When the heavy blade connects with his right side, Feo drops to his knees and rolls to the left to avoid the next slash, aimed at his neck. Gripping his wounded side, he feels the warm, sticky fluid running between his fingers, sees it dripping onto the marble floor. The mercenary looms above him, looking down with the eyes of a predator drawing first blood. As the [6]*gladius* comes down, Feo again rolls and regains his feet but cannot dodge in time to avoid a straight-on stab that delivers a slice deep into the upper leg near his groin. Then he runs as his lifeblood spills. Somehow...he runs...

Feo has run a good distance into the [8]Pasetto di Borgo at the rear of the Vatican, blood oozing from his side and pulsating from the artery near his groin, when he sees it through fading vision...a macabre yet welcome sight, sitting upright in the center of the arched passageway just ahead of him but closer this time...waiting...with unblinking red eyes. This time the familiar apparition has a voice, echoing off the walls of the corridor. "Maffeo, [9]you know me, don't you? I have need of you. If you're ready, come with me now. No more worries. No more struggle."

Feo hears his own voice as if it is coming from somewhere outside himself, for the first time in his life uttering words that are not used by an apostate. "Yes, my Lord. I know you."

He sees through me. He knows everything. He is God. He is Death. He calls and I must go. For the first time in...my life I feel...completely happy. For…the first…time in my…life I feel truly…free. For the…first time…in my…life, I…feel…peace…ful.

As his vision grows dim, Feo hears the muffled, echoing sound of heavy, running footsteps…the one who pursues him… no longer a threat…no need to run…no need to fight. Then he hears his own voice, again coming from somewhere outside himself, speaking to the rabbit. "As you have come for me, I must take leave of this life. The pain is gone. I have never felt such peace." He looks down from just above the one who kneels and slits the throat of the man lying on the passage floor.

> *My writings…at Glastonbury…Fastrada, Fastrada….*
>
> *If ever again…I place myself…in lethal straits….*
>
> *I hope…for…a more worthy cause…*
>
> *Strange but familiar…loud, explosive claps but not of thunder… and the sound of a stringed instrument amplified like a lightning bolt…wailing from a dark alley in a bleak, desperate city.*

Feo senses the presence of kindred others amidst harsh streetscapes—a trusted comrade, face painted white, and a prescient woman who is very dear. He also foresees ongoing hardships in a forsaken place where his purpose and survival methods, brutal at times, are driven not by indebtedness but by his own brand of justice and grasp of reality.

Panic-stricken and overcome by an overwhelming certainty that the worst has happened, Diggory sits paralyzed on the portico of the basilica with his back to the barred door. An undetermined period of time passes. He holds out hope that Feo will emerge, all the while knowing he will never see him again. Feo has become the closest person in his life, the son he never had. Only now does he truly grasp the depth of sorrow from the loss of a child.

Renowned Feo of Glastonbury Abbey, beloved apostate, you are everything I had ever heard you are…and so much more. Maffeo, gift of God. The remainder of my life will be a very, very long time to be without you.

⌒⌒◯

Darkness encases the campsites around the Vatican when at long last Sigeric, praying and about to give up hope, hears Diggory's deep voice speaking to the pilgrims as they approach. The image of the mountainous robed man leading loaded pack animals is distinguishable to the archbishop as they draw near. Even in the dim light, the group can make out the manner in which Sigeric is clothed. They are dumbfounded and afraid. So many unanswered questions! Although no one asks, all are acutely aware of the absence of two people—Feo and Hew. A single tear runs down Diggory's cheek as he leads the baffled group, now only three in number plus himself, quietly away from the Vatican and out of Rome in the darkness.

We arrived in Rome in full sunlight, regrettably unrecognized. We leave Rome in darkness, hopefully unrecognized. We should be well north of Ponte Molle by daybreak, keeping to long forgotten and seldom traveled pathways mapped for the archbishop's safety, thanks be to Feo.

TWENTY-ONE

13 August 990 A.D.
San Cristoforo, Italy

Fastrada's Cursed Knowing

AEMILIA AND NYSA HAVE SETTLED in comfortably. As Fastrada watches Aemilia tending to daily routines, today gathering vegetables and cooking in the taverna while her infant daughter giggles in a handmade cradle, the sight of them triggers bittersweet memories of the intrepid knight who delivered them to safety here at the sanctuary. Fastrada's thoughts of Feo are constant and disturbing, her heart and mind plagued with uneasiness, sorrow, and emptiness. Damnable knowing, an awareness of that which she could not know, plagues her consciousness.

At dusk Fastrada takes the path behind the sanctuary that leads down the steep ravine that cradles the Gordana River, the path taken by her and Feo. She makes her way to the place where she feels closest to him, the [1]Stretti di Giaredo. Taking the [2]psaltery out of the cloth sack she is carrying, she sits near the water's edge, gently strums a melody never before heard, and sings to into the *stretti*:

[3]*Ideals and virtues*
For God and for King
Both are false prophets
Your soul must take wing

Great price was paid
Death so untimely
He cries to the sea and she sings:
Life is short
Blood is cheap
Come into my arms
No need to weep

Tales of a journey
Mystical and pure
Echoed by waves
And the wind's soft allure

Float on my gales
Repose on my crests
The sea cries to him and he sings:
Life is short
Blood is cheap
I fly to your arms
And eternity reap

The last note echoes upward through the slot canyon, reverberating off primordial rock walls like many notes skittering up into the sky to dance among the stars that are appearing around a perfect Lunigiana moon. "Such a brief time together and we became one. Now begins the dreaded rest of my life without him," Fastrada laments.

[4]The stars are shining more brightly than she has ever seen them, some of them winking as if they know her thoughts, sprinkled across an indigo sky that is adorned by a luminescent full moon hanging so low and close it can almost be touched. Fastrada's heart speaks in her voice. **"Feo, a presence as strong as yours cannot simply disappear!"**

The dubious gift of prescience delivers a sudden flash of unknown however familiar, vivid scenes amidst tall buildings that line dark, dangerous streets. He walks beside her as they enter an [5]unmarked metal door and ascend stairs into a large space crowded with people in make-up and costumes. Loud music... flashing lights that create visual distortions...people's movements, jumpy and disjointed...

TWENTY-TWO

September 990 A.D.
San Cristoforo, Italy

Confirmation and Truth

¹C APPELLA DEI PELLEGRINI AND THE [2]sanctuary come into sight as the homebound travelers descend the hill above the vineyard. Diggory dreads what he feels is his responsibility, telling Fastrada of Feo's death. Leaving Sigeric and the retinue at the church, he walks the short distance across the vineyard toward the stone farmhouse. He sees Sister Aemilia crossing the north *campo* (field) with an empty sack, headed toward an apple tree. The sight of her reminds him of Feo's tight-lipped nature as he recalls how Aemilia told him, the friar, about her true identity and the heinous situation from which Feo snatched her and Nysa. At the back of the house overlooking the river, Diggory finds Fastrada removing linens from a line strung between two trees. She appears to be singing, looking downward at a laundry basket. As he gets closer, he sees Nysa's chubby arms and kicking feet, the baby lying atop dry cloths in the basket. Fastrada's song is a soft lament.

"Good day, my lady," bellows the monk as he approaches. Fastrada's expression is one of sadness and gladness to see him—but not of surprise. He senses her deep sorrow.

She knows...God in heaven...she knows.

Diggory's visit with Fastrada is short. She is stronger than he imagined, but her sorrow is beyond tears, profoundly deep, inconsolable. Before Diggory can utter a word, she tells him, "I knew you would come. I've waited to hear confirmation of my premonition before telling Aemilia." Astounded, blinking back tears, he merely says, "The remainder of our lives will be a very long time to be without him."

Fastrada asks no questions about the manner of Feo's death. She nods solemnly, and without bidding Diggory farewell, she lifts Nysa from the basket and walks across the *campo* toward the tree where Aemilia is gathering fallen apples. As he departs, Diggory looks back to see Fastrada facing Aemilia who grasps a hand over her heart and drops to her knees, her other arm around Nysa.

The first few weeks of the return journey have provided time for Diggory to answer myriad questions from the confounded travelers. Without casting suspicion or blame on anyone, he tells them of a threat against Sigeric and that Feo was killed by mercenaries when he stepped in to foil it. Diggory's response to questions about the reason behind the threat: "The archbishop's goodness and virtue are considered by some to be at odds with the pecuniary goals of opportunists within the Vatican. Let us pray that His Grace will be out of their sight once he is back in England and not foremost in the minds of those very busy people—as well as beyond their easy reach." The good monk is as kind as possible when speaking of Hew, saying only that he decided to remain in Rome indefinitely. He explains that Feo, foreseeing his own peril in countering those who would harm Sigeric, mapped out alternate roads, old Roman foot-paths, to keep the archbishop and the group unseen until they had traveled a considerable distance from Rome. The overall perception of the group, given Diggory's explanations, is that Sigeric presented the pope and those who surround him with a measure of purity they could not abide. As far as Diggory is concerned, all will be well served if Sigeric can avoid humilia-tion and maintain his dignity upon his return to England with the pallium and his title intact.

Unsurprisingly, Sigeric asks no questions about what trans-pired on that last night at the Vatican, so Diggory privately provides him with unsolicited facts, hoping the archbishop is anticipating what explanations he will provide once back in Can-terbury, especially what he will tell the abbot at Glastonbury. A raised eyebrow is Sigeric's only visible reaction to being told of Hew's involvement in an assassination plot that ultimately cost Feo his life. Hearing that Hew, believing everyone was asleep, slipped out of the retinue's sleeping quarters and was seen entering a guard's room a few evenings before the assassination attempt, the expressionless Sigeric mutters a sober response as he turns to face the surroundings, needing to look in any direc-tion other than Diggory's, "So be it." Leaving Sigeric to reflect on what has taken place, Diggory again blinks back tears as he endures the deep grief of a father.

Feo's legacy will be that of an intrepid knight, even if Sigeric the Serious chooses not to disclose the full truth about what happened at the Vatican. Chances are he will not...too much embarrassment about the lack of respect he was shown by John XV.

TWENTY-THREE

Late December 990 A.D. Glastonbury Abbey, Somerset, England

Sigeric's Untruth and Feo's Legacy

NEWS OF FEO'S DEATH HAS reached Glastonbury Abbey ahead of the archbishop, of course. Sigeric's visit with Abbot Ælfweard is discreet and unpretentious, the archbishop first offering condolences for the death of the renowned and beloved Feo, accomplished and trusted advisor of church leaders. The loss of his melodic talent and his skills at cartography and navigation are also acknowledged. Sigeric lastly expresses sincere gratitude for Feo's preparation of the route and his hunting prowess during the journey to Rome. As Diggory anticipated, Sigeric chooses not to relate the entire story, thereby avoiding any mention of the humiliating disregard shown toward him at the Vatican. He excludes any recount of the attempt by those who surround the pope, and indeed John XV himself, to eliminate him. The archbishop instead tells Abbot Ælfweard that Feo was killed inside Saint Peter's by thieves who prey upon after-hours worshipers when the basilica is nearly vacant. The abbot listens intently, all the while knowing that losing a fight with common brigands does not fit what is known of Feo's hand-to-hand combat skills. The archbishop is not questioned—nor is he believed.

A man of terse dialogue, Abbot Ælfweard acknowledges the archbishop's sincere condolences, saying, "Your Grace, we have awaited final confirmation of Feo's demise from you. Only now will we see to his personal belongings, music compositions, and writings, the latter two having untold value."

Sigeric's face and tone become more solemn than usual as he shares a long guarded secret with Abbot Ælfweard. "I say this to you only because you are one of the few remaining elders who know that the newborn Maffeo, bastard son of the revered Abbess Cynewyn of Bath Abbey, was brought here to Glastonbury to be raised as an orphan of unknown parentage. He has no remaining blood relative. I have learned that Feo's father died while he was on the journey to Rome."

With a somewhat astounded expression, Ælfweard queries, "His father?"

"Yes, his blood father," Sigeric continues. "Some battles rage in the heart with such fury that they cannot be contained in silence and secrecy. The monk Ead sought a confessor outside the walls of Bath Abbey. I was that confessor. News of his passing reached Canterbury while I was away. Ead loved Feo and was very proud of him. They met several times."

Ælfweard's expression turns to a wistful gaze. "Proud indeed, as would any man be of such esteemed progeny."

"Whatever items of value, sentimental or otherwise, that Feo left here may be considered the property of Glastonbury Abbey. However, there is a monk at Canterbury who accompanied us to

Rome. He loves Feo as a son. I leave it to your discretion whether any of Feo's belongings might be sent to him. He is a scribe and a master of weaponry. His name is Diggory." This heartwarming statement by Sigeric, the kind and humble former monk, is no surprise to Abbot Ælfweard.

⁓

Even the faithful who believe they will again meet the departed have sorrowful moments. Such is the state of the good friars at Glastonbury, some of whom have known Feo since he arrived as a newborn, raising and educating him, the beloved apostate, as he mastered many skills. They solemnly sort through the articles in Feo's quarters, finding treasures in the form of music scores and chants, poetry, and several weapons. Then Deorwine raises a leather-bound volume above his head. "Saints be praised!" The others gather around as the pages are turned to reveal a very lengthy, beautifully penned poem, an [1]untitled fantasy set in 5th century Scandinavia. It is taken to Abbot Ælfweard. Looking through the manuscript, reading parts of it, he feels awe and pride as he considers what to do.

This masterpiece is the work of a word artist. Maffeo was blessed with a gift from Cynewyn who expanded the tales of King Arthur using historical context to underpin fictional tales. The story's [1]protagonist is pagan. Yes, of course, Feo.

Ælfweard carries the volume back to Deorwine who found it. "Deliver this manuscript and Feo's [2]skeggox (Viking axe) to the monk Diggory at Canterbury."

TWENTY-FOUR

Late December 990 A.D.
¹Stretti di Giaredo and
San Cristoforo, Italy

Fastrada's Fate

"THE REMAINDER OF OUR LIVES will be a very long time to be without him." Fastrada recalls Diggory's words as she has done many times since his visit en route back to England. Her belief in ongoing consciousness, eternal entanglements, has become a comforting certainty…if only this life did not hold her prisoner in what has become an empty void.

Cursed blessing, knowing Feo! A brief taste of rapture creates fleeting hope. Once hope is gone, the remainder of one's lifetime slips into an abyss, existence devoid of joy. How can I continue to live a mere imitation of life?
Feo, a presence as strong as yours cannot just disappear!

Fastrada's thoughts ricochet off the walls of the ¹Stretti, and suddenly, in a familiar vision, they flash between abandoned buildings, along pot-holed streets in ramshackle neighborhoods, and in the littered alleys of a faraway place, a dark and dangerous city.

They are lamented in euphony in another woman's voice, channeled from the consciousness of one kindred soul to another.

Fastrada's sorrow is soul-wrenching and incessant. Long days filled with service to others at the [2]sanctuary in San Cristoforo and the *lazaretto* (house for lepers) near Arzengio are important work, but they have not lessened her grief. Heartache could be withstood for the rest of her life, but the constant emptiness, longing, and hopelessness that set in even before Diggory's visit—at the moment she felt that Feo was gone—are unbearable.

She gazes downward, scanning the striated walls of the beautiful slot canyon and the whirling water below, blue-black, inviting her, offering a gateway to eternity. Almost as if she has stepped outside herself, she observes the surroundings in free fall, plummeting in suspended time, dreamlike, watching the walls of the canyon fly past as she enters the river's merciful depths. There is an overwhelming sense of peace, not panic, as she becomes submerged beneath the water's surface, the weight of the large sandstone that is tethered to her ankle pulling her deeper, deeper. The shock of the icy water clinches every inch of her body, currents swirling around her as she is pulled downward. Bitter cold water rushes up her nostrils, delivering a sharp, stabbing pain behind her eyes, bursting upward into her forehead. She feels her windpipe close in an involuntary spasm, but the frigid [3]Gordana soon rushes into her lungs, lethal and welcome.

Please…please let death come fast! If only my chest would cease its struggling to breathe! The cold, the cold! I cannot feel my arms and legs…my heart, racing…my heart, beating so hard I can feel it in my throat, pounding through the wall of my chest and the top of my head! My heart…erratic… my heart, slow.

tthhubb...bbb…bb…b…b….

A woman's hand reaches out to Fastrada from the depths. On the wrist there is a [4]bracelet made of braided red leather strips and adorned with tiny smiling skulls. As Fastrada grasps the hand, a vivid, dynamic scene surrounds her. [5]There is loud, booming music echoing off cavernous walls and vibrating up through the floor of a crowded building in a dark and dangerous city. Fastrada can't see the city from inside this place...she just knows it's out there. People are dancing beneath flashing lights that make every movement appear to be many, disjointed. Some of the girls are naked to the waist with the nipples of their breasts covered by crisscrossed [6]gray material. Unquestionable warm ambiance. Feels like home. The woman's hand is warm and welcoming. A strong, beloved male presence is near, willfully elusive.

Aemilia is saddened but not bewildered when Fastrada does not return to the [2]sanctuary. Feo's death had plunged her into a spiritual gloom, casting an aura that encircled her. The absence of a nun's habit does not preclude the faith of a nun, and Aemilia prayed that God would give Fastrada the strength to continue her work, to find renewed purpose and happiness or at least some measure of contentment. As they talked daily, Aemilia sadly read the signs of intractable despair. Fastrada was terminally inconsolable.

Now, at this moment that she knew would come, a tear rolls down Aemilia's cheek. It was during their last conversation that she realized beyond any doubt Fastrada had lost the desire to live, that she was moving on to a metaphysical plane beyond her earth-bound existence. In Fastrada's selfless way, she spoke of the ongoing provision of lodging at the sanctuary and the comfort of *viandanti*, praising the ways in which Aemilia had stepped in to do whatever was needed. Her underlying message was that she was no longer needed here. The most ominous sign of Fastrada's resolve was when she showed Aemilia where her "leper" husband's money is hidden. She asked Aemilia to follow her to the back of [7]Cappella dei Pellegrini where she removed a loose stone in the foundation to reveal a terracotta jar, telling Aemilia she should know where it is "in the event it is needed."

Recalling tenderly the stature and character of the man who intervened to save her and her newborn, Aemilia found herself unable to question Fastrada's longing to hand over her work here and move on to an unspoken destiny. A seasoned realist, Aemilia also found herself unwilling to invoke scripture and religious teachings, finding them inadequate in the face of this depth of human despair.

My dear sister and brother, the rest of our lives—mine, Nysa's, and the lives of all who have known you—will be a long, long time to be without you. [8]*Godspeed...*

TWENTY-FIVE

December 990 A.D.
Rome, Italy

The Spider and Karma

"AROBED CORPSE DANGLING FROM the [1]*oculus* in the dome of the [2]*Pantheon* has deprived us of the amusement of watching Hew fulfill his daily penitential duties." Bishop Pietro makes no attempt to conceal his pleasure as he informs his cohorts, Vatican leaders at the *Patriarchium*, of the grisly news.

The corrupt understand better than most that one who would attempt to gain a desired position by nefarious means, such as a plot to assassinate the Archbishop of Canterbury no less, would not hesitate to do the same to others within the papacy. Such was the repute of Hew who had been under uneasy scrutiny since his decision to remain in Rome after Sigeric's departure. With the archbishop gone, Hew ratcheted up his efforts to convince Vatican officials and John XV of his value to the church, being quite outspoken about his willingness to do whatever is required to support even the most dishonorable papal intentions. His flagrant attempts at self-aggrandizement, particularly the repeated references to his past at Saint Augustine's Abbey with the renowned [3]Dunstan who reformed the English Church, became increasingly irritating to the very Vatican officials he was striving to impress. Without recognition and desperate, he continued these behaviors in spite of the fact that church leaders could not care less about anyone's illustrious past. Shameless name dropping was employed to demonstrate his self-importance with the hope that past associations with English nobility and iconic places might become avenues for achieving his less than virtuous motives. Not one to leave any potential opportunity to chance, he took the liberty of suggesting strategies to extend the greedy fingers of the Holy Roman Church into historic bastions of the Church of England and into English territories held by feudal sovereigns. The strategies all, of course, included Hew himself as the emissary of the Vatican.

"God rot the pretentious English abbot. His very presence tries my patience. If Sigeric had been killed, as attempted, and we had the opportunity to slip the abbot quickly and easily into the position of archbishop, then reach into England's resources might have been conveniently lucrative. That did not come to pass, and it is just as well now that we have experienced the irritating antics of the insufferable Hew. I have more pressing concerns involving the [4]removal of Archbishop Arnulf by French churchmen. You, Pietro, must remove the nuisance Hew from my sight!"

The order was issued, leaving open the method as to how this might be accomplished, and John XV waved Pietro away.

Under considerable pressure to carry out the pope's command, Pietro constructed a plan.

Pope John called the abbot "insufferable." That's it!

Bishop Pietro summoned Hew to inform him of his new title: Bishop, [5]Suffragan to the [6]Holy See. It took only a second, just enough time to pronounce the second word of the title, for the impact of this offensive promotion to deflate Hew's hopes and his ego.

Bishop indeed! That title becomes an oxymoron when combined with the word Suffragan. I will be used as an errand boy, a mere grunt, by those who surround the pope.

Hew's behaviors over the next several weeks deteriorated from initially submissive to groveling—more irritating than his self-important persona. Even as he groveled, he took every opportunity to impress the bishops, missing no opening while carrying out his assigned duties to point out situations that an opportunistic churchman or the papacy might wish to seize upon. The bishops attempted to keep him away from John XV by assigning him to duties within a delineated area...and then he was caught sneaking into the pope's living quarters.

"But I merely intended to apprise the Holy Father of an opportunity for the church to expand its influence in England, beginning at Glastonbury Abbey now that Feo is out of the way."

Bishop Pietro did not spend much time considering the options. He could not afford the personal consequences...not if but when...Hew would approach the pope with another proposal or create some embarrassing scene—as he most certainly would.

Idiot, am I! I should have known better than to place this sycophant into a position where he is tempted by the proximity of the pope. Yes, he is somewhat sequestered where he can be watched, and admittedly I could not resist the satisfaction of placing this arrogant fool in an embarrassing position of daily deference. The pope's voice and face when he ordered me to remove the "insufferable" Hew from his sight made it very clear that I will be held responsible. If I do not restrict him, someone other than myself will wear the mitre of the senior papal bishop. Hew has proven that allowing him to remain anywhere near the Vatican is too great a risk. The manner of his death will appear as though his role as suffragan was insufferable for him—a humiliation too great to bear.

The mercenary Bogdan dispassionately relates the Vatican's most recent paid assassination to a small group of his comrades. "The Suffragan Hew was a lucrative kill because it was not as fast and easy as a blade to the throat. It took great effort to make it appear as though he [7]took his own life. Four men scaled the sides of the [2]*Pantheon* with ropes to pull the body up the dome and drop it through the oculus. No better setting for an arrogant ass to kill himself than the highly visible, iconic pagan temple." Bogdan becomes ardent as he continues, "The worm had the audacity to boast that he designed the plan to rid the church of the lackluster Archbishop of Canterbury. He mistakenly believed we would be grateful to him for the work that the assassination provided us, adding what a foolish man Feo of Glastonbury was in disguising himself as Sigeric. I ask you, comrades, who was the fool?"

"Did you tighten the noose when he said that?" inquires one of the men.

"Aye! But not before we broke some of the [8]coxcomb's ribs and enlightened him about Feo. We lost two of our most skillful men during the encounter with Maffeo of Glastonbury. He fought fearlessly with a mere knife against three of Rome's most seasoned mercenaries and fell to a *gladius* (Roman sword) strike from behind while engaged in combat. Feo ran halfway through the Passetto di Borgo as he bled out from a severed artery. The cocky Abbot Hew did not die before hearing that Feo was indeed a formidable opponent."

In a rare moment of salute to an adversary by men who swear loyalty to no one, glasses are raised by all. "To Feo of Glastonbury."

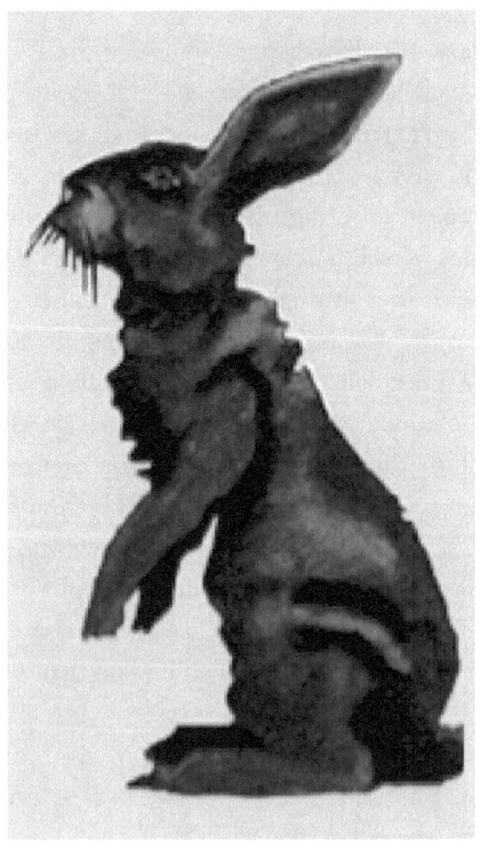

TWENTY-SIX

August 2010
Pontremoli, Italy

Epiphany

THE POSTER IS DISPLAYED IN A prominent spot at the entrance of Caffè Letterario in the Piazza della Repubblica. There will be a performance by Epifano at the ¹*Teatro della Rosa* on Saturday evening. It's him! The picture is unmistakable, shoulder-length black hair and so very handsome. He'll do a reading of selected pieces by an American poet and lyricist followed by his own music compositions inspired by the work of the same poet. The concert is titled "Memoirs de Nocturne." Niv immediately decides to attend.

It's a short walk at dusk from her apartment on Via Cavour to *Teatro della Rosa*. She heads toward the ²south-side battlement tower, turning left onto Via Ponte Battista and taking the stone footbridge across the slowly coursing, boulder-scattered ³Magra River with the ⁴Castelnuovo Tower facing her on the other side of the bridge and *Teatro della Rosa* immediately to its left. Niv can't help but ponder the stark contrast between this quaint, old-world setting and the home she recently left...Detroit to Pontremoli...surreal. The circumstances that led her here...bittersweet. The man whose performance she is about to experience, his uncanny resemblance to the conflicted, on-the-edge, fearless man she still loves...tenderly alarming. Flashes from the past—Fade grinning as she intently plucks out bass guitar lines while they listen to music, City Club and dear Goth peeps, Fade's dog Vader, and the Black Rabbit. And then suddenly from out of nowhere as she approaches the theatre entrance, she catches a fleeting glimpse of a place where she's never been, a country chapel, hears the faint sound of an ancient stringed instrument, and behind it all the sound of rushing water. At that instant, an icy chill surges through Niv's veins. She pulls the decorative scarf she's wearing up around her neck and reminds herself that it's actually a warm August evening as she enters *Teatro della Rosa* and takes her seat in one of the ⁵loges to the left of the stage. The venue is intimate, its red velvet decor a reminder of the theatre's elegant history.

The house is packed. The stage curtains are open; there will be no grand entrance. There is a simple black cloth backdrop. One acoustic guitar rests on a chrome stand next to a lone wooden stool. There is a flute on a small table to the left of the performer's stool. Minimalist, nothing to distract the audience. And a stunning surprise—the program that she was handed at the entrance says Epifano, "Fano," will perform the work of a **Detroit** poet. She suddenly feels as shaken and off-kilter as she did the night at *Carnevàle* when she first saw him.

Anxious anticipation.... It feels like I'm at a crossroads—or more likely on the threshold of an epiphany—and one that I may not want at that! My gut tells me that this whole picture—Pontremoli, the intriguing Fano, vivid flashes of unknown but familiar places and sounds, and above all the performance of the poems and lyrics of a **Detroit** *poet by this particular man, Epifano—are positive synchronicity. Go with it, Carnival, just chill and go with it.*

The sounds of people talking, taking their seats, provide a built-in alarm that interrupts Niv's mental excursion. And then the audience becomes quiet as the theatre lights dim. Niv is immediately drawn back into the moment as the crowd applauds the tall, beautiful man who is taking the stage—Fano, Pontremoli's native son and treasured artist.

He strides onstage from the left without introduction, dressed in a plain gray linen tunic, belted at the waist, over black pants. Taking a seat on the stool, he speaks to the audience with the relaxed ease of a family member. "Good evening. Thank you for being here at the lovely Teatro della Rosa as we share some time together in appreciation of an artist who lived in Detroit, an infamous American city. Before we begin, to set the tone for what you are about to hear, the words of Kiki Smith, a German-born American artist whose work focused on birth, regeneration, and the human condition: 'Artists live in unknown spaces and give themselves over to following something unknown.' The Detroit poet whose voice you will hear through his work was someone we would not otherwise know, someone whose life was short, and yet he wrote many insightful pieces about the human experience. His work is obscure even in Detroit. It was published after his death. Last year during a trip to Detroit at the invitation of a musician friend, I happened upon a book at his apartment, a collection of poems and song lyrics titled *Memoirs de Nocturne: An Anthology* by a poet and musician named simply Abe, no surname. His words rose up off the pages as I read them. In tonight's performance, you will hear his thoughts, his inner voice, in his word art. His lyrics longed for music, and now they have it. I hope he would feel that the reading and the music do justice to his work and its meaning." With that, Fano begins reading.

[6]Rebirth

Rain drops
Streak down
My window
Like shooting stars

Not symbolic sorrow
But life-giving
Inspiration
Life-giving hope

Advent of the rebirth
Reborn with the rain
Reformed with the rain
Expiating pain

Flowers cannot bloom
Without the water, giving life
Everything stops
When it's dried up inside

Not symbolic sorrow
But life-giving
Tears, tears, tears
Renewal has begun

Applause. Niv considers how the words of the poem describe her current state and the reason for her move to Pontremoli. Pausing for a moment to allow the audience to ruminate on the poet's meaning, Fano begins the second reading.

[6]Phoenix

Phoenix of fire
Sails through the ages
You know no enemy
On your stages

Bright as the stars
But you'll go higher
The Egyptians and Pharos
Called you Sire

Time is no concern
Nor restraint to your wings
Race through the galaxy
Eternity is but your slave

Messenger of destiny
The vision of worlds
You can never die
But you can never land

Time grows holes for you
Opening like desert quicksand
In a glass bottle

Again, Niv finds personal relevance in the words of the Detroit poet, Fano's masterful delivery enhancing the images, the implications—eternal hope out of ruin, immortality through rebirth. Again, the audience applauds, anticipating the next recitation.

[6]Nocturnal Talon

Cast upon high
Fly with all your might
Sail through the night
Finding life

Your wings so dark
The clouds will break
Upon your beak
Razor sharp

Your vision sure
You race the stars
Your talons clench
Upon fur

End did come fast
The fearless fowl
Flails into space
Death will pass

Again, a pause between readings. Total quiet in the theater. Darker meaning. Niv's thoughts go back to the Detroit Institute of Arts where she would meet Fade occasionally, both of them interested in the art but also because the rooms provided a quiet sanctuary where they could talk face-to-face, a place where her husband would be unlikely to look for her…unless she was followed, always a potential danger. Fano's recitations of this Detroit poet's work carry her back in time to sacred places in her memory, places still inhabited by a man named Fade who possessed a deep appreciation of the fine arts in all their forms, including the classics. And yet he lived a jungle-justice life of ruthless survival—something she simply knew about him without ever being told. She and Fade both read Dylan Thomas, and one quote always comes to mind when remembering the complex Fade, realizing he led a dual life that he kept hidden from her: "I hold a beast, an angel, and a mad-man in me, and my enquiry is to their working, and my problem is their subjugation and victory, downthrow and upheaval, and my effort is their self-expression." Fano's voice draws Niv back to the present.

[6]Sweet Irony

It stumbles on you like love
Follows you like trouble
Stabs you on the double
Those who are supposed to, never are
Ones who don't look, catch a star
Sweet irony

You were ugly in school
The kids were cruel
In the rough, you were a jewel
Ten years later, you're a queen
Those who made fun, now obscene
Sweet irony

Don't look ahead
Don't look back
Fate's is a joker
And the deck is stacked
Sweet irony

The theatre explodes in applause as Fano stands, lifts the guitar, and retakes his seat on the stool. He simply says, "Crowd Creature." The audience waits in anticipatory silence, titillated by the Detroit artist's reach and the artful delivery of their native son. Niv is transfixed as Fano glances at her...into her? It's as if he's been speaking directly to her. He begins the song with a steel-string intro, smooth and melodic, amplified naturally by the acoustics of the theatre.

6Crowd Creature

I thought I saw you for just a moment
When the eel slid down my spine
I bolted upright
And the crowd shifted tight

I looked around and I thought I saw you
I looked around and I thought I saw you

It's so cold in the middle of July
It's never been so cold, I might die
I touched myself, like frost on a rock
And bolted upright
As the eel slide down my spine

I thought I saw you for just a glimpse
As the shiver made my teeth quake
I wanted to run
But the crowd tipped over

I looked around and I thought I saw you
I looked around and I thought I saw you

It's so cold in the middle of July
It's never been so cold, I might die
I touched myself, like frost on a rock
And bolted upright
As the eel slid down my spine

Lost in reverie, as if Fade is on the stage before her, Niv again recalls how she felt during her first sighting of Fano and the meaning of this poem, "Crowd Creature."

Uncanny. Feels like an eel really did just slide down my spine. It's as if he's intentionally reaching into my past and my consciousness…Detroit poet and musician? His resemblance to Fade is remarkable, and the writings he has chosen align so perfectly with Fade's philosophy about life that coincidence seems unlikely. The poet's name was Abe. Nope, couldn't be Fade.

After several other acoustic guitar and flute compositions that were created by Fano for the poet's lyrics, he ends the night's performance with a Gregorian chant believed to have been written by a 10th century English composer, Maffeo of Glastonbury Abbey. Fano is gradually joined on stage by about 20 men and women, chanting as they approach from the rear of the theatre, slowly emerging from the aisles on each side of the audience. The smell of incense is heady, stirring. Never having heard Gregorian chanting performed live, Niv is riveted to her seat. She closes her eyes, allowing the smell of the incense and the sounds to permeate her being and soothe her spirit.

This is freaky and beautiful. I never would have imagined this combination of genres during one performance. I'm not sure how or why, but it works. It's almost as if the three artists—Maffeo, Abe, and Epifano—are existentially linked. Yep, Niv, you've flipped out.

Niv waits just inside the door of the theatre, hoping she can keep her nervousness in check, summoning the courage to talk to Fano when he walks out. "Why?" she asks herself, quickly rationalizing that she must speak with him because of the Detroit connection, which is actually the least important of two reasons. She's almost afraid to mention the primary reason because he might think she's bat-shit crazy. Twenty minutes pass. They're locking the doors, so she moves outside and waits near the old masonry wall between the pedestrian walkway in front of Teatro della Rosa and the river. Street lamps cast an amber glow on the theatre and the nearby steps leading up to a small park. "Good," she tells herself. "This wait has allowed me to compose myself and get my thoughts together." She waits for another ten minutes. Just as she has given up and begins to walk away, Fano steps out the door with a guitar case slung over his shoulder. He immediately acknowledges her, cocking his head to the left with a wry smile as he walks toward her. His shoulder-length black hair has been pulled back into a ponytail. His easy, friendly manner is no surprise after tonight's performance and his warm interactions with the audience. Not waiting for Niv to speak, he extends a hand and says, "I saw you in the loge tonight. Thanks for coming."

Handsome, yes. Fade, no. Differences around the nose and mouth. More outgoing, more sociable, but he's not living the life of a Goth, a creature of darkness in an urban wasteland. A few years older, faint crow's feet at the corners of his eyes, piercing green, unlike Fade's brown. Sprinkling of gray in his hair. Ever so subtly feminine in his mannerisms but more so in his sensitivity. His voice, soothing. But what am I foolishly looking for? Fade is dead. This man is Epifano.

"I enjoyed the performance very much and couldn't resist hanging around to meet you. My name is Niv. I'm a native Detroiter."

———

The next few days find Niv and Fano together, getting to know each other during [7]*passeggiate* (evening strolls) on the stone streets of Pontremoli. Her favorite walks are through the evocative [8]Piagnaro neighborhood with its [9]*surchetti* (narrow lanes) leading uphill to [10]*Castello del Piagnaro* and across the [11]*Ponte di San Francesco di Sotto*, the less traveled footbridge over the [12]*Parco della Torre* at the end of Via Cavour. The park provides a peaceful escape from the throngs of people during [13]*Medievalis*. A medieval history lesson shared by Fano is revealing. His strong opinions about the unjust subjugation of the masses by the wealthy, the church, and emperors spew forth as he explains Pontremoli's distant past and the opposing factions, the [14]Guelphs and the [14]Ghebellines, who divided the town into the upper town, the [14]Sommoborgo, and the lower town, the [14]Imoborgo. "There were powerful nobles, some with lawful authority and some with religious authority. When they weren't feuding with each other, they combined efforts to advance their greedy causes. Neither situation resulted in good for struggling commoners."

The sound of water gently rushing over sandstone rocks in the river beside the park is soothing, almost as if its purpose is to provide the atmosphere for tender dialogue and the unfolding of a story...or perhaps just seemingly related circumstances that will never be understood? Fano and Niv are aware of their mutual bewilderment. He was struck immediately by her looks the night when they first spoke outside Teatro della Rosa...jet black hair with bangs cut straight just above her eyebrows, black tea-length dress, over-the-ankle boot heels, flawless make-up but not too much, and a unique red braided leather bracelet with little smiling skulls. Looking at her now, he is reminded that she seemed hauntingly familiar that night and even more so as he has come to know her better. Conversations are easy and deep. Fano is very curious about Niv's life in Detroit, especially her past with Fade—the humanist, rogue, realist, Goth purist, and social warrior.

How I wish I could have known him, but I feel as though I do know him through Niv's experiences...and beyond that. It's weird in a good way, familiar and welcoming. It all feels connected somehow but beyond my understanding. Déjà vu-ish...and familiar...like I felt when I first read the work of the Detroit poet Abe. He and Fade — contemporaries and both dead. And Niv, the bewitching Niv. She has walked into my life a kindred spirit, like a longtime lover or a long lost sibling.

Fano isn't alone in his intense curiosity. "How did you happen to find the poet's work in Detroit?" Niv inquires.

"It was on the coffee table in the apartment of the musician who invited me to stay with him. There was also a novel by the same author. It was very graphic and contained brutal scenes, but even so the stream of consciousness passages spoke to me. I'm drawn to the work of obscure artists, such as the ancient chant by Maffeo of Glastonbury Abbey that was performed during the concert at Teatro della Rosa. So it was with the lyrics of the Detroit artist." Pausing briefly, Fano recounts his introduction to the Detroit poet's work. "I tried to contact Abe for permission to use his work. For some unknown reason, he never used a surname, making it extremely difficult to find him. No one knew much about him, including the musician I was staying with. He told me he knew Abe briefly. They were in a heavy metal band together. Abe was the lead singer and had co-written some of the songs. He disappeared mysteriously, and the word among my friend's small circle of [15]*amici* (friends) was that he was killed in a shootout with rogue cops in a bar on Detroit's southwest side. His written work showed up later. I went to a public library to see if anyone there might know something about Abe or who might own the rights to his work. They had one copy of the novel and one copy of the collection of prose and lyrics. Only one librarian knew anything at all about how the books were obtained. The author apparently had turned his work over to an underground publisher who felt it was worthy of posthumous publication. Abe had requested that, in the event his work was published, the books be donated to that specific library."

Alarms are going off in Niv's head.

Killed in a shootout with rogue cops in a bar in southwest Detroit?!

Already knowing the answer, she asks, "Was that library on Library Street at Gratiot Avenue?" Suspecting what Niv is certain of, Fano nods as [16]an eel slides down their spines.

TWENTY-SEVEN

Early Autumn 2010
Pontremoli and
San Cristoforo, Italy

Tapestry

IT'S A WARM AND COMFORTABLE RELATIONSHIP, Fano and Niv growing more and more fond of each other. No expectations, no strings, just middle-aged people from different cultures on different continents enjoying those differences during an ongoing dialogue about music, art, their lives, and the human condition. He is pleased to learn that she plays bass guitar, encouraging her to buy one and also to pursue her craft, creating Goth jewelry with her signature braided leather and tiny smiling skulls. She's learning about his life here in the region known as Lunigiana, fascinated by the natural fit of this man with this special place. They have enduring, intimate conversations the likes of which Niv has had only with one other person, the darkly fascinating Detroiter Fade. The relationship between her and Epifano is mutually fulfilling, Niv in particular feeling grateful for his presence in her life. Through him, she has learned Fade's real name and his sustained gifts and legacy—his writing. Synchronicity. It must be the reason she was drawn to this mystical place.

It's a perplexing tangle of thoughts and emotions that one has in a survivor's existence. You are left alive, breathing, thinking...damnable thinking and bittersweet remembering. Healing is not an option and is actually objectionable. That leaves only finding another way to live and breathe until I die. Epifano, meaning revelation of God, is here and now, a gift. I only hope I can give him a fraction of the joy and comfort that I find in his company.

Niv finds herself in a good place emotionally, her juvenile whimsy again calling forth the storyline of a favorite childhood tale, wondering if she's been granted a second adventure in [1]Neverland. Fano has a rebellious streak, just enough to be constructive, a man of the people. He has eclectic interests without boundaries, continually delving into provocative topics. He is combative, not with his hands, but with words and principles. His appetite to learn about the urban wasteland that is Detroit, and more specifically its Goth heyday, is voracious. Now it's clear why he was dressed as he was when she first saw him at *Carnevale*. His curiosity about her relationship with Fade is respectful and non-intrusive. Fano is totally devoted to music and the fine arts, another reminder of someone dear. Likewise, Niv is told by Fano that she shares the characteristics of someone...a person he can't tag with a name, place, or time. He refers to Niv as "a young, lovely [2]*Befana* (a woman who delivers gifts to children throughout Italy on Epiphany Eve)," observing that she also seems to be aware of what has happened or will happen, including things about him that she couldn't possibly know. Niv has discovered, by piecing together sections of Fano's narrative and through intuition, that his life is intentionally loose-ended. She's certain there has been a stream of women...and men...through his bedroom. Even during the most intimate encounters with him, there's an impenetrable barrier around his being. *Déjà vu* — like Fade, a man who will never commit sole fidelity to her or anyone. In spite of this, he is without question the warmest human being she's ever known.

⌒⌒⌒

It's a short ride up the hill outside Pontremoli to San Cristoforo, a tiny settlement where [3]*Cappella dei Pellegrini* (Chapel of the Pilgrims) is located. Fano has mentioned the chapel several times, and today he has impulsively decided to come here. It would be easy to miss the tiny country church amidst vineyards below the road. As they descend the hill, Niv's thoughts are on how she has arrived at this place, at this time in her life. The better she has come to know Fano, the more she's aware of synchronicity and convinced of predestination…that what she was told by the doctor in Detroit, to pay attention, was advice about ongoing connections, entangled consciousness. She's grateful for the advice and that she tuned in, willing to recognize the phenomenon when it presents itself.

Fano is not Fade, but they are somehow connected, just as I must be connected with each of them and others in a [4]cyclorama that is perpetual—past, present, and future.

The old church is small and quaint, its rock walls and roof showing centuries of wear and tear. Part of the roof has been repaired, perhaps hundreds of years ago, by overlapping slabs of slate, apparently without regard for its original slope. This irregularity only adds to its charm. There's a palpable soul here.

It's no wonder Fano likes this place. He's convinced of its connection with Maffeo, the obscure 10th century composer whose chant he used as the finale of the performance at Teatro della Rosa.

Fano has told Niv how he found the chant among others as he sifted through fragile old manuscripts in a room off one of the [5]cloisters at [6]*Chiesa della Santissima Annunziata* in Pontremoli. The music had been recopied many times over the centuries and is believed to have arrived here by way of church hands from an abbey in England. By whatever means they traveled, the time-worn scores found their way to Pontremoli and were lying there as if waiting to be discovered by someone who would bring the beautiful chants to life. Fano has also shared the history, possibly folklore, about the composer with Niv. Maffeo, known as Feo of Glastonbury Abbey, is believed to have accompanied the Archbishop of Canterbury on a pilgrimage to Rome during which they stopped at *Cappella dei Pellegrini* in 990 A.D. They were given respite at the stone farmhouse, having skirted around Pontremoli to avoid roadway tolls.

Strolling the perimeter of the church, there is a steep drop-off at the rear and side of the building where Niv hears the sound of water far below. As if triggered by the sound, she experiences a sudden vision of a [7]slate-roofed stone house on the other side of the church. When they round the church and reach the front door, the sight of the stone house is no surprise. Slowing her pace, taken aback by the familiarity of the surroundings, Niv tells Fano, "Pardon the pause. The witch is having a flash." He readily understands, tilting his head slightly to the left and giving her a familiar grin. Standing at the church entrance facing the stone house across a small [8]*campo* (field), Fano tells her. "You aren't alone, [9]*la mia buona strega* (my good witch). I've heard things here at the door of the chapel, a woman singing, almost as if she's weeping at the same time, accompanied by a stringed instrument." Niv squeezes his hand.

It's a short walk across the vineyard to the stone house that once belonged to the church. The earth has a tilled appearance, clumps of dirt turned up in random patches, causing the walkers to detour around the disrupted areas. Niv gives Fano an inquisitive look as she points at the condition of the ground. He explains, "*Cinghiali*. Feral pigs have been rooting here." Over the hillside drop-off that extends alongside the church and behind the stone house, a [10]river can be seen below, trickling around large rocks. The sounds of a dog barking and sheep bleating far below blend with the swooshing of water running through the valley…primeval. The shadow of a long forgotten and almost indistinguishable path, a lesser known leg of the ancient [11]Via Francigena, clings to the side of the steep slope just out the back door of the stone house. It is apparent why the house, in whatever its original state had been, was used as a *refugio* (shelter) for pilgrims who skirted around Pontremoli to avoid tolls and prayed at the *Cappella dei Pellegrini*.

"Now for today's most strenuous adventure," Fano declares as he smiles gleefully and motions Niv toward an overgrown footpath that veers off the Via Francigena between the stone house and the old chapel, leading down a steep descent to the river. He adds, "Good thing it's unseasonably warm. The water at the canyon is cold even on the hottest summer days." All Niv can think of is snakes as she and Fano make their way downward through the dense, jungle-like vines and undergrowth. Once at the river it takes about an hour of walking and climbing over rough, rocky river banks to reach their destination. What lies at the end is worth the hike! The [12]Stretti di Giaredo, a natural wonder, appears before them like a setting in a dream. A dream? Again, the surroundings are hauntingly familiar to Niv. The canyon, the old church, the stone farmhouse…Fano…it's as if the [4]cyclorama of places, people, and happenings that she has seen again and again since that fateful night with Fade in Detroit has reached full circle here in this primordial place…a colorful tapestry of her life…entwined with others past and present.

"I'm going to pass," she tells Fano as he strips off his shirt and pants before tiptoeing into the frigid water. "Something tells me you won't stay in there very long." He shivers as the [13]tattoo of a black rabbit on his right side disappears below the water, a tattoo that Niv has seen before and has not asked him about, but she will….

This may or may not be another [1]Neverland, but it is where I belong for now… fatefully [14]entangled.

Ending Note

WE'VE SEEN THE MAN WHO resembles Abe in Pontremoli many times since he first appeared in the Piazza della Repubblica on that sunny July morning in 2016. More than a year after first seeing him, with the help of some liquid courage, I approached him in a restaurant where he was sitting with friends and told him of his resemblance to my son. In a kind and gentle voice, he asked to see a photo of Abe on my phone which he passed among the others at the table. He and his friends immediately put me at ease in the warm manner of the Pontremolese.

Perhaps it was just a random occurrence that a flesh-and-blood messenger appeared before us to inspire this story, but I think not. Whatever the reason, Stefano, your presence is a gift.

Sally Sulfaro

We all shine on
Like the moon and the stars and the sun

Instant Karma
John Lennon

Stone farmhouse referred to in *Co-eternals* as "The Sanctuary," located next to the Chapel of the Pilgrims in San Cristoforo just outside Pontremoli, Italy

Annotations

Pre-sequel Background

[1] Goth is short for Gothic, a subculture that began in England during the early 1980s among the followers of Gothic rock, an offshoot of the post-punk genre. Rock artists associated with the shaping of the subculture include Siouxsie and the Banshees, The Cure, Joy Division, and Bauhaus. Goth styles of dress draw on punk and new wave as well as Victorian and Edwardian. Some Goths wear combinations of all of these. The preferred fashion color is black with pale faces and black hair, but Goths are not just people who think it's cool to wear black. In general, they do not see fitting into mainstream society as a healthy or worthwhile pursuit and are more likely than most people to value experience, intellect, and knowledge above other characteristics. They value honesty, integrity, and personal style and disdain fake people referred to as "posers" and "wannabes." Some Goths have hedonistic tendencies related to drugs and sex while many are serious about their careers and supporting their families. Goths defend friends and family, readily stepping in to handle a violent or threatening situation such as in the diner scene in Chapter 47 of *The Antiheroes* when the protagonist Fade and his Goth friends take social justice to unjustifiable lengths in defense of a geeky Goth kid. The subculture has continued to draw adherents decades after its appearance with crossover into Emo music and the dress and make-up of its devotees. The Goth subculture as it existed in Detroit during the 90s and continued into the following decade is considered by some to have been the city's golden age of Goth. It is a central concept in the novel *The Antiheroes: Treatise of a Lost Soul* by Abe Sulfaro (1970-2014), known to some who knew him as the Gothfather.

Chapter 1: Fade Away

[1]Small provincial city within a region known as Lunigiana (Land of the Moon) in northern Tuscany. Pontremoli has also been called Porta dell'Apennino (door to the Apennines) due to its strategic position at the junction of the Magra and Verde Rivers at the foot of the Apennine Mountains, providing natural defenses. Pontremoli was referred to as Puntremel by Sigeric, Archbishop of Canterbury, when he stopped here in 990 A.D. en route to Rome. The birth of the settlement is obscure, although the presence of Ligurian people in its early history is certain. Literally translated, Pontremoli means "trembling bridge" (from the Latin *pons tremulus*), believed to have been named after a prominent bridge across the Verde River. It is unclear whether there was a rickety bridge in the town at one time, and the bridge or town may have been named after a popular wood that was used for building. The town became a nexus in the development of Italian publishing. Generations of booksellers have gone forth from this area to sell books on the countryside and in the town squares of northern Italy. Each summer in Pontremoli there is a ceremony, the *Bancarella,* during which booksellers from across the country reward bestselling books. Ernest Hemingway was awarded the *Premio Bancarella* (Book Stall Prize) for *The Old Man and the Sea* at the first *Bancarella* in 1953.

[2]Fortress dating to the 10th century, built to control access to several passes over the Apennine Mountains, routes into the Magra Valley. The castle originated around a tower erected in the 10th century by the Longobarda deli Adelberti family, a branch of the Obertenghi dynasty, on Molinatico Mountain's meridional hill in defense against Hungarian attack. The structure has undergone numerous demolitions and rebuildings over the centuries due to sieges and derives its name from the sandstone slab plates (*piagne*) common in the area and used to cover houses. At the time of this writing, Piagnaro Castle houses the stele sandstone statues, icons of Lunigiana, the oldest statues dating to 5,000 BC, evidence of a prehistoric people. The castle dominates the town of Pontremoli from a hill overlooking the main piazzas (Piazza della Repubblica and Piazza Duomo) and is reached via *surchetti* (narrow lanes) branching off Via Garibaldi and winding through an evocative jumble of medieval buildings known as the Piagnaro neighborhood.

[3]In *The Antiheroes*, the main character Fade has a black rabbit that he believes has special powers, particularly the ability to predict his death. He

likens his Black Rabbit to the Black Rabbit of Inlé, the grim reaper of the rabbit world in Richard Adams' novel *Watership Down*.

[4]See Pre-sequel Background, annotation #1 describing Gothic ("Goth") subculture.

Chapter 2: The Black Rabbit's Call

[1]Leland City Club located on Bagley Street, Detroit, believed to be one of the largest Gothic Industrial nightclubs in the world during its hey-day (late 1990s through half of the first decade of 2000s). It is a central location and favorite night spot of the protagonist Fade and his Goth comrades in *The Antiheroes: Treatise of a Lost Soul* by Abe Sulfaro. The club exists behind an unmarked black metal door off the parking lot of the Leland Hotel.

[2]From this point to the end of this chapter, content is from *The Antiheroes: Treatise of a Lost Soul* by Abe Sulfaro.

[3]From this point through "kindred hands..." the content was added by S. Sulfaro.

Chapter 3: Old World Allure

[1]Town; village. Also historically used to refer to a larger geographic area such as a region or country. Pontremoli is sometimes called the "Door to Tuscany," being located at the northernmost point of Tuscany. In ancient times, pilgrims, armies, and merchants traveled on the Via Romea (Via Francigena) en route to Rome. Pontremoli continues to be a stop on that route, a strategic location where the Magra and Verde Rivers converge. The town's name is from the Latin "pons tremulus" meaning "trembling bridge," believed to refer to an ancient wooden bridge. Pontremoli is in a region known as Lunigiana, Land of the Moon.

[2]Ancient pilgrims' route across Europe, also known as the Via Francigena, leading to Rome. Although the route was used for centuries before Sigeric, Archbishop of Canterbury, documented the route in stages in 990 A.D., prior records were sparse. There were actually many different routes due to vary-ing points of departure across Europe, seasonal road conditions, and politi-cal situations impacting passage through certain regions, giving rise to the expression "All roads lead to Rome." Some pilgrims continued their journeys to Jerusalem.

Chapter 4: Straddling Two Worlds

[1]A physical phenomenon that occurs when particles such as photons inter-act in a manner that results in transmission of a discrete amount of energy, proportional in magnitude to the radiation frequency of each individual par-ticle and not independent of the other(s), is transmitted—even when sepa-rated by great distance. Quantum state must be considered as a whole system. If one particle in a pair is acted upon, the other particle "knows" even though there was no means of communication. The result is an unknown amount of impact on the entire system. Particles can be in two places at the same time (superposition). Once entangled, particles are inextricably linked. Albert Einstein referred to quantum entanglement as "spooky action at a distance." He didn't like it because the math describing the quantum wave provides no help in predicting results. Einstein and others such as the renowned physicist Niels Bohr studied this phenomenon in the 1930s, coming ever closer to an understanding of it in the 1950s. Quantum entanglement is still mysterious but is known to be a real phenomenon. Recent scientists tell us that nature itself "knows" about entangled particles and that entanglement does not nec-essarily happen at great distance. If current quantum mechanics is correct as the phenomenon relates to consciousness, neither of two entangled particles knows which way it will be oriented until it passes through a filter that is believed by some to be the human brain (neocortex), but the fate of one particle reveals the fate of the other. Of great interest to the author of *Co-eternals* is the potential correlation between quantum entanglement and the ancient Akashic records believed to be a compendium of all human events including our thoughts, emotions and words of the past, present and future (a cyclorama) that exist on a non-physical etheric plane. It is hoped that mate-rialistic science (physics, chemistry, biology) is evolving to a higher under-standing of the connection between the physical substance of the brain and the non-physical human mind (consciousness). That evolved understanding could bring science and consciousness, indeed science and faith, into align-ment and harmony.

[2]Narrow lanes through a jumble of medieval stone buildings compris-ing Pontremoli's Piagnaro neighborhood leading upward to Castello del Piagnaro.

[3]An area of old-world stone buildings on narrow lanes (*surchetti*), most of them jutting off Via Garabaldi and ascending to Castello del Piagnaro.

[4]Fortress dating to the 10th century, built to control access to several passes over the Apennine Mountains, routes into the Magra Valley. The castle originated around a tower erected by the Longobarda deli Adelberti family, a branch of the Obertenghi dynasty, on Molinatico Mountain's meridional hill in defense against Hungarian attack. The structure has undergone numerous demolitions and re-buildings due to sieges over the centuries and derives its name from the sandstone slab plates (*piagne*) common in the area and used to cover houses. At the time of this writing, Piagnaro Castle houses the stele sandstone statues, icons of Lunigiana (Land of the Moon) and proof of prehistoric inhabitants of the region, the oldest statue dating to 5,000 BC. The castle dominates the town of Pontremoli from a hill overlooking its main piazzas (Piazza della Repubblica and Piazza del Duomo) and is reached via *surchetti* (narrow lanes) branching off Via Garibaldi and ascending through the Piagnaro neighborhood.

[5]A 62-kilometer (39-mile) river that runs through Pontremoli and several other towns and villages in northern Italy. In Roman times, it was known as the Macra and marked the eastern border of the territory of Liguria.

[6]A community theatre first established in 1767 after Pontremoli passed from Spanish rule to the Grand Duke of Tuscany. The Academy of the Rose ensured the theatre's financing and cultural livelihood with the support of twenty-five of Pontrtemoli's most affluent families. Teatro della Rosa is an architectural gem. Original decorations were extremely refined. Damage was endured during WWI and WWII, leaving only the beautiful scene curtain as a surviving remnant of its historic decor. The theatre continues to stage events, concerts, meetings, and conferences and is the symbol of cultural life in Pontremoli.

Chapter 5: The Abbess

[1]A collection of Old English annals tracing the history of the Anglo-Saxons. The original manuscript was created in the late 9th century.

[2]Latin for *History of the Britons*; believed to be a history of the indigenous British people written around 828 AD. It survived in the form of numerous recensions dated after the 11th century. The work has been attributed to Nennius because some recensions contain a preface written in his name, but some experts believe the Nennius preface to be a forgery and argue that the *Brittonum* is actually an anonymous compilation.

[3]Pope John XII occupied his position 955-964 AD. He was a corrupt and sacrilegious pope who toasted Satan during a drinking spree and put his notorious mistress/prostitute in charge of his brothel in the Lateran Palace, an ancient Roman building that later became the main papal residence (*Patriarchium*) in southeast Rome.

[4]Referred to as churl in some sources. Early Anglo-Saxon middle and lower middle class of freemen, some quite poor. Free and slave were the two overarching social categories. The noble class was known as thegn.

Chapter 7: The Archbishop's Summons

[1]Sigeric became Archbishop of Canterbury following the death of Æthelgar on February 13, 990 A.D.. Æthelgar had been the archbishop for less than two years following the death of the renowned Archbishop Dunstan on May 19, 988 A.D. It was an unstable period for the English crown with Æthelred the Unready (King of the English 978-1013 A.D.), a weak and unpopular monarch, taking the crown at 13 years of age after his mother, Queen Ælfthryth, ordered her servants to kill 15-year-old King Edward. Edward, who subsequently became known as Edward the Martyr, was her stepson, crowned at 12 years of age following the death of his father, King Edgar. In 991 A.D., the strategically inept Archbishop Sigeric advised Æthelred the Unready to pay tribute to the Danish king, Sweyn Forkbeard, to avoid invasion. The result was increased Danish demands and *danegeld* (taxes) being imposed on the inhabitants of the English territories. Arguably as the result of the precedent set by bad advice he had given the king, Sigeric paid tribute to the Danes later the same year to prevent the burning of Canterbury Cathedral. Æthelred launched a massacre of Danish settlers, resulting in further invasions by the Danes into England. This demonstrates the interrelationship between church and crown, their shared involvement in national and political affairs, and the impact of concurrent incompetent leaders, King Æthelred and Archbishop Sigeric. In areas where there was weak secular leadership, the opportunistic papacy could advance its greedy intentions. Whether a secular or religious leader was in power, the poor underclasses were no better off in either case. Known as Sigeric the Serious, his pilgrimage to Rome in 990 A.D. was the first to be mapped showing 80 stages.

[2]John XV was pope 985-996 A.D. He was unpopular because of his venality and nepotism. He split the church's finances among his relatives. He was known to be corrupt and gained money by dishonorable means.

³The ecclesiastical jurisdiction of the Catholic Church in Rome.

⁴Official stopping places on Roman roads; shelters.

⁵ Plural of *viandante*; travelers, wayfarers, or pilgrims. Italian: *pellegrini.*

⁶The ancient Pilgrim's Way, also known as the Via Francigena, stretching from multiple starting points across Europe to Rome. One of the routes was referred to as the Frankish Route (*Iter Francorum*) in the *Itinerarium Sancti Willibaldi* of 725 A.D.. Many routes from various origins led to the familiar saying, "All roads lead to Rome."

⁷Stringed instrument with a long neck having frets. A lute has a shape like a halved egg and is played by plucking the strings.

⁸Medieval round-backed, stringed instrument that was strung with gut and played with a plectrum made from a quill or carved from horn; ancestor of the guitar.

Chapter 8: Delicate Strategies

¹Dormitory; sleeping quarters.

²Dining hall; refectory.

³Meeting room.

⁴Record of the travels of Willibald, Bishop of Eichstatt of Bavaria in 725 A.D.. It mentions the *Iter Francorum* (Frankish Route), later known as the Via Romea or the Via Francigena.

⁵Pilgrims made stops along their routes at sites where they honored local saintly persons and purchased "relics" which were souvenirs or keepsakes. The relics were taken home as proof not only of the pilgrim's piety, but also that he/she had actually made the pilgrimage.

⁶Rural land properties that were the basis for the division of fiefdoms.

⁷Old English phrase meaning "by Christ's fingernails," considered to be sacrilegious because the words were believed to actually affect God's body in heaven. Catholics believed that when a priest uttered words during communion, a crust of bread literally became God's physical body, such as bones and flesh, broken and eaten.

⁸Stopping places, particularly on old Roman roads. Some were simple encampment sites. The word *mansio* is from the Latin word *manere* meaning "to remain" or "to stay." They were also called *spedali* (Italian, plural) or *spedale* (Italian, singular).

⁹Present day Sombre in Wissant, France located just across the English Channel.

[10]Purse.

[11]Stages on Sigeric's journey were actually documented during the return trip from Rome to Canterbury. The 80 *mansios* or stages have since been numbered in both directions. Prior to Sigeric's journey in 990 A.D., there was no clearly described route.

[12]Person who keeps and disburses money and food.

[13]Meat, usually pork, slow cooked in oil at a low temperature and stored in jars in fat to repel water and create a seal. This method preserved meat for months.

[14]Storage area for ale and wine; word from the old French *boterie* and Latin *botaria,* meaning cask or bottle.

[15]An abbey in Canterbury, England that was reorganized by Dunstan to conform with Benedictine Rule. Dunstan, who had been an abbot at Glastonbury Abbey, was Archbishop of Canterbury 959-988 A.D. He restored monastic life to England and reformed the English Church. Dunstan was canonized as a saint in 1029 A.D.

[16]Tall hat that looks like a pointed arch; headdress worn by bishops and senior abbots as a symbol of their office.

[17]Hood sewn into the neck of a monk's robe.

[18]Rural parish.

[19]Present day Berceto, Italy.

[20]Eighth century Bishop of Rennes (ancient capital of the Duchy of Brittany) in France (Gaul). Moderanno was later patron saint of Berceto, Italy near Cisa Pass. Folklore has it that while on a pilgrimage to Rome, Moderanno was given relics of San Remigio and was to deliver them to the pope. He forgot them during a stop at Cisa Pass on the Via Francigena where they were left hanging on a tree branch. Upon his return, the tree had grown very tall, the branch holding the relics so high they could not be reached. Moderanno promised that he would donate them if they could be reached, and the tree lowered the relics to him.

[21]Wrote *Confessions in Thirteen Books* in Latin between 397 and 400 A.D. in which he describes regrets about leading a sinful and immoral life and about his conversion to Christianity in which Saint Ambrose had a role. He authored *Rule of Augustine* which outlines life in a religious community, citing core virtues of chastity, poverty (perfect charity), and obedience. Several texts from Letter 211 were borrowed by Benedict for insertion into his Rule of Saint Benedict.

²²Bishop of Pavia, 680 A.D. Damian decried monothelitism (the belief that Jesus Christ has two natures, human and divine, but only one will), as opposed to dyothelitism (the belief that Christ has two wills). Monothelitism was denounced as heresy at the Third Council of Constantinople in 681 A.D. Damian was known for his ministry to the poor and the sick and is said to have healed a leper with a kiss.

²³Originally located on an island 43 kilometers above surrounding terrain near Arles in Provence, France. It is the legendary sanctuary of Saint Trophimus who was sent from Rome by Saint Peter to convert the Gauls. He took shelter there in a cave around 46 A.D. There is a rock cell under the church that is called The Confessional of Saint Trophimus. A legend holds that the island is the gravesite of some of Charlemagne's soldiers.

²⁴Site of the Church of Limoges founded by Saint Martial, Apostle of Aquitaine, who was sent from Rome and became bishop 250-251 A.D. He is buried there. It is also the home of Saint Valerie who was beheaded for her faith during Roman times.

²⁵Holy shit (Old English).

²⁶In January 897 A.D., one year after the death of Pope Formosus, his body was removed from its tomb and put on trial by order of Pope Stephen VI (sometimes referred to as Stephen VII). Formosus was accused of perjury and also of illegally acceding to the papacy. His rotting corpse was strapped upright in a chair and questioned by Stephen VI. A deacon read the answers that had been written by Stephen. Formosus was found guilty and his papacy retroactively declared null. The corpse was stripped of its ecclesiastical vestments and three fingers were cut off the right hand, the fingers that were used during his lifetime for blessings. The body was then placed in a graveyard designated for foreigners but was later dug up and thrown into the Tiber River with weights tied to it.

²⁷The Dark Ages of the church from 904 to 964 A.D., also referred to as Reign of the Whores, Rule of the Prostitutes, Reign of the Harlots, and the Pornocracy. It began with Pope Sergius III and ended with Pope John XII. During this period, popes were under the influence of the corrupt, aristocratic Theophylacti, a family that included a woman named Theodora and her daughter, Marozia. Theodora ruled as a queen. Marozia was the mistress of Sergius III. The women ruled using beauty and wealth and carried out their power plays through male surrogates, ergo the fable of a female pope. Marozia had many lovers and married Guy of Tuscany in

order to join forces and successfully carry out a *coup d'état* against Pope John X who was jailed in Castel Sant 'Angelo where he died, reportedly smothered with a pillow by Guy of Tuscany. Marozia had her son by Sergius III installed as Pope John XI when he was 21 years of age. Her nephew, son of a younger sister, became Pope John XIII. It was during the papacy of John XII, also a member of the Theophylacti family, that the Lateran Palace (home of the popes, also referred to as the Patriarchium, in the south of Rome) was considered a place of depravity and referred to as a brothel. John XII died during an adulterous sexual encounter, either from a stroke or killed by the woman's husband, depending on the version of the story one chooses to believe.

[28]Monastery's administrative meeting rooms.

[29]Bishop's staff that symbolizes the shepherd of God's flock.

Chapter 9: The Apostate and the Monk

[1]France.

[2]Lily of the valley.

[3]Present day Bar-sur-Aube, France.

[4]Ergotism, also known as St. Anthony's Fire, is a condition that can progress to gangrene, vision problems, spasms, convulsions, and unconsciousness after grain infected with the fungus *claviceps purpurea* is ingested.

[5]Present day Brienne-le-Chateau, France.

[6]Forty days before Easter; period of fasting and abstinence from meat. Black Fast additionally limits food intake to one post-sunset meal per day without meat, wine, dairy, oil, eggs, butter, or cheese.

Chapter 10: A Father's Heart

[1]Latin. Dark Ages during which time the pontificate was corrupt under the influence of the Theophylacti family (904-964 A.D.); also called the Rule of the Harlots, the Rule of the Whores, and the Pornocracy. History has recorded the powerful involvement of two voluptuous imperial women, Theodora and her daughter Marozia, referred to as "papal whores." Papal vice included murders, brothels, adultery, conspiracies, nepotism, and simony (the selling of ecclesiastical items, favors, titles, and positions). More detail in Chapter 8, annotation #27.

[2]One who has fallen away from or denounced religious beliefs.

Chapter 11: Alpine Perils

[1]Mountain pass at an elevation of 8,100 feet connecting Martigny in the canton of Valais, Switzerland with Aosta, Italy, its lowest point on a ridge between Mont Blanc and Monte Rosa, the two highest summits of the Alps. The pass is located on the main watershed between the Rhone and the Po Rivers and was used as early as the Bronze Age and later by the Romans, the Celts, and Napoleon.

[2]Mountain pool or lake formed in a cirque excavated by a glacier. In the Great St. Bernard Pass, tarns do not support a habitat suitable for fish.

[3]Wild plant having an anise-like scent when crushed; also called Queen Anne's Lace. The leaves of the unflowered plant are similar to hemlock leaves. The differences between cow parsley and hemlock are slightly hairy stems on cow parsley, the hollow stems of hemlock, and the pleasant parsley and anise-like smell of cow parsley when crushed.

[4]Highly poisonous plant used for nefarious purposes. Greek philosopher Socrates was sentenced to death by consuming a hemlock-derived drink. More detail in Chapter 16, annotation #6.

Chapter 12: Saints and Sacrilege

[1]Town near present-day Tremello, Italy. Pavia dates to 89 B.C. when it was a Roman settlement.

[2]Author of the Rule of Saint Augustine, circa 400 A.D., that outlined life in religious communities including the core virtues of chastity, poverty (perfect charity), and obedience. His writings expressed intense remorse for sexual sins and stressed the importance of sexual morality.

[3]Also known as Saint Damien, Bishop of Pavia, 680 A.D., born into Italian nobility and known for his learning and piety. He wrote a letter against monothelitism (view that Jesus Christ has two natures but only one will) to Emperor Constantine IV in 679 A.D. to mediate relations between the Lombards and Byzantine emperors on behalf of the Archbishop of Milan.

[4]Area of a monastery or religious community where money is distributed.

[5]A place where church officials meet with visitors.

[6]Plant of the genus *mandragora* whose roots are hallucinogenic and narcotic. In higher doses, it induces unconsciousness, so it was used as an anesthetic for surgery in ancient times. Mandrake is found in England

and around the Mediterranean. Further described in Chapter 14, annotation #13.

[7]The hub or main area of a church.

Chapter 13: Mystics and Murders

[1]Present day Montelungo within the Comune of Pontremoli (medieval: Puntremel), Province of Massa Carrara; stage 49 on Sigeric's itinerary.

[2]Land of the Moon; a natural corridor linking Europe with the Italian peninsula and connecting the Po Valley with the Tyrrhenian area. Historic Lunigiana covered the diocese of Luni, a Roman city founded at the mouth of the Magra River in the 2nd century B.C. and known to have been inhabited during the Bronze Age.

[3]Present day Pontremoli, Italy at the foothills of the Apennines and Cisa Pass (Passo della Cisa) where ancient routes connected the Po Valley with Liguria and Tuscany. Pontremoli (Puntremel) was first mentioned in Sigeric's 990 A.D. travelogue.

[4]Piagnaro Castle built by the Longobardo deli Adalberti family, a branch of the Obertenghi dynasty (see annotation #5), in the mid-10th century as a defense against Hungarian attacks. It overlooks the Via Francigena (Via Romea) and Pontremoli. The structure now contains a museum exhibiting megalithic sandstone stele statues (4000-1000 BC) that originated in the area surrounding Pontremoli. One of the oldest statues was found at San Cristoforo, a settlement on the outskirts of Pontremoli.

[5]Family dynasty with a stronghold in Ormala near Piacenza. The Obertenghis crossed the Apennines in the 10th century to become the first liege lords of Lunigiana, dividing the territory into over forty small fiefdoms where they built castle fortresses, some remaining to present day. Lunigiana's divisions belonged to wealthy families such as the Obertenghi dynasty but also the church and its bishops (Bishops of Luni). The Longobardo deli Adalberti family, credited with building Piagnaro Castle, is a branch of the Obertenghi dynasty, Adalbert being the son of Obert I of Luni. The noble Malaspina family emerged from the Obertenghi dynasty during the 12th and 13th centuries.

[6]Excommunication ritual signifying outcast status for life. Lepers (people with Hansen's disease, leprosy) were considered socially dead long before

physical death. Relatives inherited a leper's property. Lepers were removed from the community and were often housed in places called lazarettos.

[7]Present day Arzengio remains meagerly populated. It was settled by ancient pagan soldiers, farmers, and shepherds who were late to adopt Christianity.

[8]Roman road design; main branch runs north-south. See #9 below.

[9]Roman road design; secondary branch runs east-west. The perpendicular crossing of the *cardo* and the *decumanus* was usually the location of the town's center.

[10]Stringed instrument of the zither family dating to ancient Greece; used in Europe from the 10th through the 15th century.

[11]Doorhead; lintel; crosspiece over a door or window carrying the weight above it.

[12]Talisman; magic symbol to keep evil spirits from entering, such as a gargoyle on a church.

[13]Pilgrim. Plural: *viandanti*.

[14]Latin meaning "Entrance not of the enemies," i.e. friends are welcome.

[15]Multipurpose sheriff who collects taxes and census information, enforces laws, and keeps vassals working to reduce lost time in farming; might also act as judge and sentence criminals.

[16]Cisa Pass (Passo della Cisa) marks the border between the Ligurian and Tuscan Apennines near the source of the Magra River. It is at 3,414 feet above sea level.

[17] Italian word for pilgrims.

[18]Titular commander assigned to a border province of the Holy Roman Empire or a kingdom. In some areas of Europe, the position became hereditary. The first Margrave of Lunigiana was Obert I of Luni (974 A.D.) followed by his two sons, Adalbert I and Obert II. The Malaspina family of Lunigiana descended from Obert II.

[19]Present day *Cappella dei Pellegrini* in San Cristoforo, Italy with stone farmhouse next to it referred to as "The Sanctuary."

[20]Stone farmhouse still standing near *Cappella dei Pellegrini* in San Cristoforo.

[21]Small settlement above the right bank of the Gordana River approaching Pontremoli from the north. One of the oldest of the megalithic stele statues was discovered here in 1948.

²²Gordana River located in western Lunigiana. The river runs near *Cappella dei Pellegrini* and the stone farmhouse in San Cristoforo.

²³Wild boars.

²⁴Leviticus 26:7.

²⁵John 6:12

Chapter 14: The Sanctuary and the Black Rabbit

¹Small settlement above the Gordana River just outside Pontremoli, Italy.

²Comune in northern Italy where the Magra and Verde Rivers converge in the region known as Land of the Moon (Lunigiana); medieval name Puntremel. The name Pontremoli is most commonly believed to mean "trembling bridge."

³Chapel of the Pilgrims near a stone farmhouse ("the sanctuary") in San Cristoforo just outside Pontremoli (medieval: Puntremel), Italy. The country church is located on a lesser traveled branch of the Via Francigena (Via Romea) believed to have been used to avoid tolls that were charged to pass through Puntremel.

⁴Stone farmhouse next to *Cappella dei Pellegrini* in San Cristoforo, Italy.

⁵Refuge; hostel; lodging for pilgrims

⁶Field.

⁷Wild boar.

⁸Pilgrims.

⁹Mountain pass in northern Italy marking the division between the Ligurian and Tuscan Apennines at an altitude of 1,040 meters (3,414 feet) above sea level near the source of the Magra River that flows through Pontremoli.

¹⁰Small village bordering Pontremoli in northern Italy.

¹¹Lunigiana (Land of the Moon), a region in northern Tuscany where Pontremoli and San Cristoforo are located.

¹² Last rites; eucharist (communion) that ensures the dying that they die with Christ who promises them eternal life.

¹³*Mandragora officinarum*, genus name Latinized from two Sanskrit words for "sleep" and "substance," also known as Satan's Apple. The root often resembles human form, resulting in a belief in alleged aphrodisiac properties. Mandrake produces a state of unconsciousness and was used for its anesthetic properties during surgery in ancient times. It has been associated with superstitious practices throughout history. This plant has more folklore written about it than almost any other.

[14]Quote from author/poet Abe Sulfaro in *Memoirs de Nocturne.*

[15]Pilgrims.

[16] Poem title "Sweet Irony" in *Memoirs de Nocturne* by Abe Sulfaro (1970-2014).

[17]House used to separate people with leprosy (Hansen's disease) from society; also called a pest house or leprosarium. Some quarantine sites were endowed with income from bishops and abbots using income from tithes, rent, and tolls. Unlike some other regions in Europe, lepers in northern Italy were considered a civic responsibility.

[18]Gordana River in western Lunigiana that enters a narrow canyon, the Stretti di Giaredo. The Gordana flows through San Cristoforo directly behind and below Cappella dei Pellegrini and the stone farmhouse referred to as "the sanctuary."

[19]Stretti di Giaredo, a gorge/slot canyon with walls more than 50 meters high on the Gordana River in western Lunigiana. The canyon has been described as a natural rock vagina that reminds one of the origin of the world or an ancestral place of worship.

[20]Advanced syphilis, a venereal disease, was often mistaken for leprosy because of its similar signs and symptoms. Both conditions were believed to be caused by an immoral soul. Leprosy in particular was considered punishment for lechery and other sins. Both conditions can progress to death.

[21]Purse.

[22]Black rabbit, death muse of the main character Fade in *The Antiheroes* by Abe Sulfaro who credits British author Richard Adams' Black Rabbit of Inlé in his dark fantasy *Watership Down.*

[23] "Uht" is an Old English word for the time just before sunrise when mist hangs heavy over fields and lakes and the last few stars can be seen.

[24]From the poem "Crowd Creature" in *Memoirs de Nocturne* by Abe Sulfaro.

[25]Stringed instrument of the zither family dating to ancient Greece; used in Europe from the 10th through the 15th centuries.

Chapter 15: Roadway Rogues

[1]Saint Dunstan lived 909-985 A.D.. He was at Saint Augustine's Abbey in Canterbury, later becoming Abbot of Glastonbury Abbey and lastly Archbishop of Canterbury. He is credited with reforming the English Church and applying Benedictine Rule in order to restore monastic life to England. Dunstan was canonized in 1029 A.D..

[2]Hostel; *ospedale*; hospital. The Altopascio *spedale's* purpose was caring for pilgrims, and it became known far and wide. Even pregnant women traveled there for childbirth. The Order of the Knights of Tau, the earliest Christian institution to combine military protection with assistance to pilgrims, was founded there in 1070-1080 A.D.. Brothers and friars of the order wore long black coats bearing the awl-shaped Taumata cross. Their role later expanded to include safeguarding roads and bridges from brigands, making the roads southward toward Florence and Rome free of heavy tributes and maintaining a ferry over the Arno River. Original parts of the *spedale* at Altopascio later became the apse and bell tower of the church San Jacopo Maggiore.

[3]Wild boar.

[4]Garments or robes worn by clergymen.

[5]Meat, usually pork, slow cooked in oil at low temperature and stored in jars in fat to repel water and create a seal. This ancient method preserved meat for months.

[6]The importance of Luca (now Lucca), where Altopascio is located, was diminishing during the late 10th century. It was replaced by Florence as the Margravate of Tuscany. Lombard rule was replaced by Frankish rule in 990 A.D.

[7]Under dual oversight by the Holy Roman Emperor and the Pope, Christendom was supposedly a singular order, however this was not borne out in reality. The Emperor was the Christian monarch, having moral guardianship of the church and only indirect rule over countries. This arrangement created role confusion, reflected a quasi-religious purpose on both fronts, and resulted in power struggles between pope and emperor.

Chapter 16: The Spider's First Bite

[1]Present day Montefiascone, Italy.

[2]Also known as common nettle or scrub nettle, botanical name *urtica incisa*. The plant grows wild in Europe, Asia, northern Africa, and western America. Its leaves and stems have hollow hairs (trichomes) that inject histamine and other substances, causing an electrifying, burning sensation. Natural remedies include dandelion, spores on the undersides of ferns, and lemon juice.

[3]Pope John XV was known for venality and nepotism. He split the church's finances among his relatives and was described as corrupt, gaining money through dishonorable means.

[4]Stretti di Giaredo, a gorge/slot canyon with walls more than 50 meters high on the Gordana River in western Lunigiana. The canyon has been described as a natural rock vagina that reminds one of the origin of the world or an ancestral place of worship.

[5]The original untitled manuscript of *Beowulf* was written by an anonymous Anglo-Saxon author and is believed to have been written between 975 and 1025 A.D. The untitled Old English epic poem came to be known by the name of its pagan protagonist. It appears to be based on oral history and created for entertainment using historical backdrops. Dating of events has been confirmed by archaeological excavation. The story is set in 5th century Scandinavia where Beowulf defeats a demon and its vengeful mother. The hero becomes a king, is killed in a battle with a dragon, and a tower is erected in his memory. *Beowulf* may be the oldest surviving poem written in Old English. It is the longest with 3,182 lines. The manuscript was badly damaged in a fire at Ashburnham House in Westminster in 1731 and suffered further damage by handlers in subsequent years. It is now held by the British Library.

[6]Poisonous plant with white flowers that develop into green, ridged fruit containing seeds. The leaves and the fruit are highly lethal, causing initial loss of speech and respiratory distress. An early sign is excessive salivation and drooling followed by small muscle twitching progressing to full paralysis. Death is caused by asphyxia after cessation of respiratory function. Hemlock does not bring a peaceful death because the person is conscious as breathing ceases. Hemlock has a bitter taste and mouse-like odor. Socrates was sentenced to death by drinking hemlock.

[7]Æthelred (The Unready), King of the English, was crowned at 13 years of age after his mother, Queen Ælfthryth, arranged the murder of her stepson, 15-year-old King Edward who became king at the age of 12 following the death of his father, King Edgar. This resulted in Æthelred's unpopularity and the murdered Edward being named Edward the Martyr. Æthelred proved himself to be an ineffectual ruler, taking bad advice in 991 A.D. from Sigeric, Archbishop of Canterbury, to pay tribute money to the Danes in order to avoid invasion. The result was increased Danish demands and taxes (*danegeld*) on the inhabitants of English territories. It also resulted in Sigeric paying the Danes to prevent Canterbury Cathedral from being burned. Æthelred launched a massacre of Danish settlers, causing further invasions into English territory.

[8]Papal corruption was well known and has been described in multiple sources. *Antapodosis*, written by Bishop Liutprand of Cremona, contains a papal history of vice among popes and their episcopal colleagues between 886 and 950 A.D. Until the 11th century, popes called themselves "ecumenical patriarchs." There are multiple sources describing what is referred to by papal historian Cardinal Caesar Boronius (1538-1607 A.D.) as the Rule of the Whores during the 10th century, also called the Pornacracy in another source. Excesses and widespread wickedness in the Christian clergy included the sale of ecclesiastical appointments, deceit, scandals, immorality, fraud, murder, and cruelty. On more than one occasion, the papacy was sold to rich and aristocratic families. The church's secular arm forced dogma on humanity, sometimes through mass murder, with clergy carrying out the functions of local authorities of the state. Much unsavory papal history was recorded in *Diderat's Encyclopedie* published in 1759, but it was ordered destroyed by Pope Clement XIII.

[9]Tall, pointed headdress worn by bishops as a symbol of their title.

Chapter 17: Spins the Spider

[1] Ancient bridge, also known as Ponte Milvio (Milvian Bridge), across the Tiber River (the Tevere.) The bridge has been rebuilt many times and is the oldest bridge in Rome, originally built by Gaius Claudius Nero in 206 B.C. In 63 B.C. this bridge is where the letters of conspirators were intercepted and then delivered to Cicero at the Senate. In 312 A.D. the famous Battle at Milvian Bridge was a crucial point in a civil war that ended with Constantine I as sole ruler of the Roman Empire and established Christianity as the empire's official religion. In 1849 the bridge was badly damaged by Garibaldi's troops in an attempt to block a French invasion.

[2]Old Saint Peter's Basilica was erected during a 30-year period in the 4th century A.D. by order of Emperor Constantine I, the Roman Empire's first Christian emperor, at the base of Vatican Hill on the west bank of the Tiber River where Saint Peter is believed to have been martyred and buried. The original structure resembled Roman basilicas and audience halls with gabled, pointed roofs and without the lavish exterior of earlier pagan temples. The present day domed basilica was built over a 100-year span with completion in 1506 A.D.

[3]Towering cylindrical building on the right bank of the Tiber River in Parco Adriano in Rome. Originally the Mausoleum of Hadrian, it was built

between 134 and 139 A.D. It became a military fortress in 401 A.D. In 590 A.D. Gregory the Great, praying for an end to the Justinian Plague, had a vision of Archangel Michael sheathing his sword over the castle, signifying the end of the plague and inspiring the name of the castle. Pope Leo IV ordered the building of the Passetto di Borgo circa 850 A.D. It is an arched passageway connecting Castel Sant'Angelo with the oldest section of the walls enclosing the Vatican.

[4]Tiber River, generally flowing southerly with Rome on its eastern banks.

[5]Large residential complex in southern Rome where popes lived until the 14th century. The complex included the Basilica of Saint John in an area known as Laterno, at Saint John's Square on the Callian Hill, and was protected by an ancient Roman wall. It is also known as the Lateran Palace or *Lateranense Palatium* and more formally as the Apostolic Palace of the Lateran. The basilica was occupied during the early Roman Empire by the Laterani family who served as administrators for several emperors. There was a period of six decades, culminating with the papacy of John XII, who became pope in 964 A.D. at the age of 18, that has been referred to as the Pornocracy. John XII was known for adultery, fornication, and incest (his niece), turning the Lateran Palace into a virtual brothel.

Chapter 18: Humiliating Reception

[1] Bishop's staff signifying the shepherd of God's flock.

[2]Tall, pointed granite structure, 25.5 meters high, still standing at the Vatican on the spot where it was erected after it was brought to Rome from Egypt on the order of Emperor Caligula in 37 A.D. See Chapter 20, annotation #7 for more detail.

[3]Also known as the Lateran Palace, located in the southern part of Rome; papal residence until the 14th century. The palace was referred to as a brothel during the Reign of the Harlots, also known as the Pornocracy or more delicately as the *Saeculum Obscurum* (Dark Ages) beginning in 904 A.D. and lasting until 964 A.D.. Also described in Chapter 17, annotation #5.

[4]Pope John XV was known for venality and nepotism. He split the church's finances among his relatives and was described as corrupt, gaining money through dishonorable means.

[5]Chivalric Catholic monastic military order that was instrumental during the Crusades and predating the Knights Templar.

Chapter 20: Feo's Fate

[1]Woolen vestment conferred by the pope on an archbishop.

[2]Old Saint Peter's Basilica, not the present structure, would have been standing during the time this story takes place. The original church was built in the 4th century by order of Emperor Constantine, the Roman Empire's first Christian emperor, on the spot where Saint Peter was believed to be buried. The church resembled Roman pagan basilicas and audience halls, having a pointed, gabled roof, five aisles, and a wide central nave. Its capacity was 3,000 to 4,000 people. The present domed structure was built in the 15th century.

[3]Central aisle or main body of a church or basilica; area accessible to non-clergy.

[4]In *The Antiheroes: Treatise of a Lost Soul* by Abe Sulfaro, the Black Rabbit is the protagonist's death muse. Sulfaro credits the concept to English author Richard Adams with the origin of the Black Rabbit of Inlé in the novel *Watership Down* (1972).

[5]Mercenaries, soldiers of fortune who would fight battles and kill for money or other compensation, were used from the time of Julius Caesar. They were often Germanic barbarians who were paid to protect Roman frontiers. The world's most feared forces consisted of freelance warriors, glorified killers who sold their skills to the highest bidder and changed sides at will. One such group, the White Company, fought both for and against the pope, for and against the city of Milan, and for and against the city of Florence. When there was no war, they raided towns and villages. In 1506 A.D. a company of Swiss soldiers of fortune became papal bodyguards and Vatican watchmen. This continued even after Switzerland forbade its citizens from being mercenaries. Those bodyguards and watchmen have evolved into the present elite Swiss Guard.

[6]Plural of *gladius*, the primary sword of ancient Roman foot soldiers.

[7]Red granite, 84-foot-tall Egyptian structure still standing in Saint Peter's Square directly in front of the basilica. It was originally erected at Heliopolis, Egypt circa 2500 B.C. by an unknown pharaoh. Roman Emperor Augustus had the obelisk moved to Alexandria, Egypt around 30 B.C. It was moved to the Circus of Caligula (Circus of Nero) in present-day Vatican City, by Caligula in 37 A.D. where it presided over Nero's brutal games and Christian executions. The obelisk has been in its current location at the Vatican since 1586 A.D.

[8]Pasetto di Borgo, also known as Corridore di Borgo, is a passageway within the oldest surviving section of the walls enclosing the Vatican. Constructed of archways, the Pasetto links Saint Peter's Basilica with the ancient Castel Sant' Angelo (originally the Mausoleum of Hadrian, built 135-139 A.D. as described in Chapter 17, annotation #3). The Pasetto is believed to have been intended as an escape route between the Vatican and the castle. Parts of the passage were built by Totila, King of the Ostrogoths, during the Gothic War (535-554 A.D.), but were poorly built and crumbled. In the early 9th century, Charlemagne King of the Franks and first Emperor of the Holy Roman Empire, crowned by Pope Leo III, decreed the building of a new wall on which the passageway was later constructed. The Passetto was fully erected as a walkway in 1277 A.D. by Pope Nicholas III.

[9]From this point in the narrative through the set of italics (Feo's self-talk) following it, the dialogue is a modified version of protagonist Fade's self-talk as he is dying in *The Antiheroes: Treatise of a Lost Soul* by Abe Sulfaro.

Chapter 21: Fastrada's Cursed Knowing

[1]A breathtakingly beautiful slot canyon with striated rock walls more than 50 meters high on the Gordana River in western Lunigiana. The canyon has been described as a natural rock vagina that reminds one of the origin of the world or an ancestral place of worship.

[2]Stringed instrument of the zither family dating to ancient Greece; used in Europe from the 10th through the 15th centuries.

[3]Song lyrics titled "Sea Knight" written by Sally Sulfaro for Champion Eternal, a rock group formed by Abe and Josh Sulfaro and Marty Fitrzyk. The lyrics were never used and were found among Abe Sulfaro's poetry, lyrics, and notes following his death.

[4]Land of the Moon, an area in northern Italy.

[5]Leland City Club on Bagley Street in Detroit, Michigan, believed to be one of the largest Gothic Industrial nightclubs in the world during its heyday from the late 1990s through half of the first decade of 2000s. City Club is a central location and favorite night spot of the protagonist Fade and his rogue Goth comrades in *The Antiheroes: Treatise of a Lost Soul* by Abe Sulfaro. The club exists behind an unmarked black metal door off the parking lot of the Leland Hotel.

Chapter 22: Confirmation and Truth

[1] Italian for Chapel of the Pilgrims.

[2] Stone farmhouse referred to as "the sanctuary," still standing next to *Cappella dei Pellegrini* in San Cristoforo, Italy.

Chapter 23: Sigeric's Untruth and Feo's Legacy

[1] The original untitled manuscript of *Beowulf* was written by an anonymous Anglo-Saxon author and is believed to have been written between 975 and 1025 A.D.. The Old English epic poem came to be known by the name of its pagan protagonist. It appears to be based on oral history and created for entertainment using historical backdrops. Dating of events has been confirmed by archaeological excavation. The story is set in 5th century Scandinavia where Beowulf defeats a demon and its vengeful mother. The hero becomes a king, is killed in a battle with a dragon, and a tower is erected in his memory. *Beowulf* may be the oldest surviving poem written in Old English. It is the longest with 3,182 lines. The manuscript was badly damaged in a fire at Ashburnham House in Westminster in 1731 and suffered further damage by handlers in subsequent years. It is now held by the British Library.

[2] Single-handed Viking (old Norse) axe used for hand-to-hand combat and for throwing. The lower portion of the axe bit is called the "beard," a hook used to pull weapons out of opponents' hands and to pull down their shields.

Chapter 24: Fastrada's Fate

[1] Beautiful slot canyon of striated rock on the Gordana River near Pontremoli and San Cristoforo in northern Italy.

[2] A stone farmhouse still standing next to *Capella dei Pellegrini* (Chapel of the Pilgrims) in San Cristoforo on the outskirts of Pontremoli and near the Stretti di Giaredo on the Gordana River.

[3] Gordana River that runs through western Lunigiana (Land of the Moon) in northern Tuscany.

[4] The handmade bracelet worn by Niv at City Club in Detroit in *The Antiheroes* by Abe Sulfaro.

[5] The largest Goth industrial club in the United Sates, possibly in the world, in the '90s and early 2000s. City Club is in a hidden location behind an unmarked door off the parking lot of the Leland Hotel in Detroit, Michigan.

Co-eternals

[6]Duct tape was used to meet the required minimum cover for females who chose to attend topless at Leland City Club. The tape was worn crisscrossed over the nipples.

[7]Chapel of the Pilgrims, a small country chapel next to a stone farmhouse ("the sanctuary") on an obscure leg of the Via Francigena in San Cristoforo, a small settlement on the outskirts of Pontremoli, Italy.

[8]Expression of well wishes to someone who is beginning a journey.

Chapter 25: The Spider and Karma

[1]Circular opening 27 feet in diameter in the center of the *Pantheon* dome. Some experts believe the *oculus* was designed to function as a giant sundial when the original edifice was built by Emperor Hadrian in 128 A.D. The opening, which is the only source of light within the building, was oriented to cast a single sunbeam each midday and also to illuminate the doorway on the equinoxes as well as on April 21, the anniversary of the founding of Rome. It is also believed that the *Pantheon*'s representation of the passage of time was intended to emphasize the divine power of the emperor. See annotation #2 for further detail about the *Pantheon*.

[2]2,000+-year-old (27 B.C.) pagan temple considered to be one of the most architecturally sophisticated Roman structures with the largest unreinforced concrete dome in the world. As the name *Pantheon* implies, it was originally built as a temple to all the gods. The *Pantheon* is located in Rome's Piazza della Rotonda and has the monumental tombs of historic figures, including the artist Raphael and two kings of Italy, Vittorio Emanuele II and Umberto I, set into its walls.

[3]Dunstan was the abbot at Glastonbury Abbey and a key figure in the reformation the Church of England in accordance with the Rule of St. Benedict. He revered Augustine and changed the dedication of the Church of Saint Peter and Saint Paul in Canterbury, established in 578 A.D., to include Saint Augustine. From 978 A.D. forward it became known as Saint Augustine's Abbey. Dunstan became Archbishop of Canterbury in 959 A.D. and remained in that position until his death in 988 A.D. He was canonized as a saint in 1029 A.D.

[4]In 991 A.D. there was a serious dispute over the removal of Arnulf, Archbishop of Reims, France who was the illegitimate son of King Lothair. The removal, carried out by French churchmen, took place at a synod that Arnulf

had refused to attend and during which he was deposed for alleged high treason. He was replaced by Gerbert, a humanist, scientist, scholar and teacher. Pope John XV intervened by sending a legate to preside over a second synod during which Gerbert was suspended and Arnulf reinstated. Arnulf was ultimately found guilty of treason, and Gerbert later became Pope Sylvester II.

[5] A bishop who assists another bishop of higher rank.

[6]The pope and the officials of the Vatican, comprising a sovereign entity. Holy See also refers to the ecclesiastical jurisdiction of the Catholic Church.

[7]Suicide in medieval times was generally a private act, concealed by those who committed it and considered too terrible to talk about. Only the suicides of men, such as those of higher station and favorites who had fallen from grace, were likely to be made public, especially in religious and monastic settings.

[8]Insulting name for a vain, foppish person. The cockscomb on the top of a cock's head is used for arrogant displays, strutting, and looking self-important.

Chapter 26: Epiphany

[1] The theatre is an architectural gem. The Academy of the Rose, established in 1767 after Pontremoli passed from Spanish rule to the Grand Duke of Tuscany, ensured Teatro della Rosa's financing and cultural livelihood with the support of 25 of Pontrtemoli's richest families. Original decorations were extremely refined. Damage was endured during WWI and WWII, leaving only the beautiful scene curtain as a surviving remnant of the theatre's historic decor. The most recent renovation was in 1998. Teatro della Rosa continues to host events, concerts, meetings, and conferences and is the symbol of cultural life in Pontremoli.

[2]Torre del Casotto, a 12th century structure.

[3]A 62-kilometer (39-mile) river that runs through Pontremoli and several other towns and villages in northern Italy. In Roman times, it was known as the Macra and marked the eastern border of the territory of Liguria.

[4]A 12th century tower that was part of the defense system and used as a gated entrance into the town.

[5]Private boxes on the sides of a theatre at the level of the first balcony.

[6]From *Memoirs de Nocturne: An Anthology*, a posthumously published compilation of the poems, song lyrics, novel excerpts, and quotes by Detroit musician, author, and poet Abe Sulfaro.

[7]Plural of *passeggiata*, often stated as *passeggiata serale*, a traditional slow evening stroll after the harsh summer sun has gone down.

[8]A jumble of old-world stone buildings on narrow lanes (*surchetti*), most of them jutting off Via Garabaldi and ascending to Castello del Piagnaro.

[9]Narrow stone lanes.

[10]Fortress dating to the 10th century, built to control access to several passes over the Apennine Mountains, routes into the Magra Valley. The castle originated around a tower erected on Molinatico Mountain's meridional hill by the Longobarda deli Adelberti family, a branch of the Obertenghi dynasty, in defense against Hungarian attack. The structure has undergone numerous demolitions and rebuildings due to sieges over the centuries and derives its name from the sandstone slab plates (*piagne*) common in the area and used to cover houses. At the time of this writing, Piagnaro Castle houses the stele sandstone statues, icons of Lunigiana (Land of the Moon) and evidence of prehistoric inhabitants of the region, the oldest dating to 5,000 B.C. The castle dominates the town of Pontremoli from a hill overlooking the main piazzas (Piazza della Repubblica and Piazza del Duomo) and is reached via *surchetti* (narrow lanes) branching off Via Garibaldi and winding upward through the Piagnaro neighborhood.

[11]Ponte della Stemma (Bridge of the Coat of Arms), a south-side stone footbridge bridge also known as the Bridge of San Francesco Sotto (under) to distinguish it from the Bridge San Francesco Sopra (over) at the north end of the town. Via Della Cresa leads from the upper footbridge at the base of the hill that is dominated by Piagnaro Castle toward the lower footbridge beside Torre del Casotto, also known as Tower Seratti, beside the Magra River.

[12]Park of the Tower beneath Ponte della Stemma (Bridge of San Francesco Sotto) on the bank of the Magra River.

[13]Annual four-day medieval festival that takes place in August in Pontremoli.

[14]Lower town (south), Imoborgo during the 13th and 14th centuries, is marked by Via Cavour, ending at a 12th century structure, the Torre del Casotto. Upper town (north), Sommoborgo during the 13th and 14th centuries, is marked by Via Garabaldi. Opposing factions were the Guelphs who swore allegiance to the papacy and the Ghibellines who were aligned with the Holy Roman (German) Emperor. The factions occupied the two separate sections of the town with Il Campanone, the Big Bell, as the central part of a fortress marking the division between Imoborgo and Sommoborgo. Il

Campanone, a tower erected in 1322, still stands overlooking the Piazza della Repubblica.

[15]Plural of *amico*, Italian for friend.

[16]Song lyrics by Abe Sulfaro titled "Crowd Creature" in *Memoirs de Nocturne*.

Chapter 27: Tapestry

[1]Mystical, fictitious place where an ageless boy named Peter Pan, the Lost Boys, Tinker Bell, and the Darling children experienced the most fantastic adventures of their lives in a story written by Sir James Barrie (1860 – 1937), Scottish novelist and playwright.

[2]According to Italian tradition, a benevolent old woman riding a broomstick fills children's shoes with candy and presents on the night of January 5.

[3]Italian for Chapel of the Pilgrims.

[4] Scene showing 360 degrees and observed from the inside. There is no beginning or end. It is circular, cyclic.

[5]Plural of cloister (from Latin *claustrum*), a covered but open gallery or arcade, typically monastic Italian, running along the walls of a building and forming a quadrangle.

[6]Prominent church in Pontremoli erected in the 15th century at the will of a doctor named Princivalle Villani following the sighting of an apparition of the Virgin at a shrine where the Annunciation (announcement of the Incarnation by Gabriel) was frescoed. The church has two cloisters.

[7]Stone house with slate roof referred to as "the sanctuary," still standing next to *Cappella dei Pellegrini* in San Cristoforo, Italy.

[8]Field.

[9]Italian for "my good witch."

[10]The Gordana River where the Stretti di Giaredo is located. It flows behind *Cappella dei Pellegrini* and the stone house (the sanctuary) in San Cristoforo.

[11]Via Francigena, the common present-day name for the old Via Romea, also called The Pilgrim's Way and The Frankish Route. There were many roads through Europe, all leading to Rome from various starting points and changing as needed to avoid harsh roadway conditions, ergo the saying, "All roads lead to Rome."

[12]Gorge / slot canyon on the Gordana River in western Lunigiana with walls more than 50 meters high. The canyon has been described as a natural

rock vagina that reminds one of the origin of the world or an ancestral place of worship.

[13]Quote from Fade, the main character in the novel *The Antiheroes* by Abe Sulfaro: "If I were an animal totem spirit, I would be a black rabbit. I always wait for his call. Death is a constant companion for all of us, and I have the Black Rabbit tattooed on my right side."

[14]Refers to quantum entanglement, a physical phenomenon that occurs when atomic particles such as photons interact in a manner that transmits a discrete amount of energy, proportional in magnitude to the radiation frequency of each individual particle and not independent of the other(s)— even when separated by great distance. Quantum state must be considered as a whole system. If one particle in a pair is acted upon, the other particle "knows" even though there was no means of communication. The result is an unknown amount of impact on the entire system. Particles can be in two places at the same time (superposition); therefore, time is not necessarily linear or chronological. Once entangled, particles are inextricably linked. Einstein referred to quantum entanglement as "spooky action at a distance." He didn't like it because the math describing the quantum wave provides no help in predicting results. Einstein and others such as the renowned physicist Niels Bohr studied this phenomenon in the 1930s, coming ever closer to an understanding of it in the 1950s. Quantum entanglement is still mysterious but is known to be a real phenomenon. Recent scientists tell us that nature itself "knows" about entangled particles and that entanglement does not necessarily happen at great distance. If current quantum mechanics is correct as the phenomenon relates to consciousness, neither of two entangled particles knows which way it will be oriented until it passes through a filter that is believed by some to be the human brain (neocortex), but the fate of one particle reveals the fate of the other. Of great interest to the author of *Co-eternals* is the potential correlation between quantum entanglement and the ancient Akashic records believed to be a compendium of all human events including our thoughts, emotions and words of the past, present and future (a cyclorama) that exist on a non-physical etheric plane. It is hoped that materialistic science (physics, chemistry, biology) is evolving to a higher understanding of the connection between the physical substance of the brain and the non-physical human mind (consciousness). That evolved understanding could bring science and consciousness, indeed science and faith, into alignment and harmony.

www.ingramcontent.com/pod-product-compliance
Lightning Source LLC
Chambersburg PA
CBHW030114260626
47156CB00008B/2649